Sixteen After Ten

First published by Lilian Press 2008

Sixteen After Ten gratefully acknowledges
the generous financial support of the School of English, TCD.

ISBN 978 0 9555025 4 5

Cover design, text design and typesetting by Anú Design
Printed and bound by ßetaprint, Dublin 17, Ireland

Sixteen After Ten
Oscar Wilde Centre for Irish Writing
21 Westland Row
School of English
Trinity College Dublin
Dublin 2
REPUBLIC OF IRELAND

For information on the M. Phil. in Creative Writing
visit www.tcd.ie/OWC
For information on other masters programmes offered by the School of English visit
www.tcd.ie/English/index.php

Sixteen After Ten

New writing from the Oscar Wilde Centre
Trinity College Dublin

Staff

Acknowledgements

The authors of *Sixteen After Ten* would like to thank: the School of English, Trinity College Dublin; Gerald Dawe, Deirdre Madden, and Lilian Foley of the Oscar Wilde Centre; our writer fellows Brian Lynch and Mary Morrissy; and our lecturer Jonathan Williams. Their support and encouragement has made this publication possible.

Contents

Gerald Dawe ✦ *Foreword* ix

Viv McDade ✦ *Tidal Pool* 1

John Holten ✦ *Valhalla: Some Scenes in Foreign Spaces* 13

Emily Firetog ✦ *What We Remember in Forgetting* 23

Mary Turley-McGrath ✦ *Poems* 37

Charlie Stadtlander ✦ *The Smoking Car* 47

Monica Strina ✦ *The Privilege* 59

Naoimh O'Connor ✦ *Roosters* 69

Philip St John ✦ *The Road to Valerie* 79

Carmen Cullen ✦ *Love, Love Me Do* 91

Rachelle Dolan ✦ *Trees* 101

Niall Duff ✦ *The Topaz Bistro* 115

Ruth Patten ✦ *What Was Lost* 127

Maria Pace ✦ *In Between Dreams* 137

Mark Stewart ✦ *Does Not Compute!* 145

Phyl Herbert ✦ *Lunar Ladies* 157

Andrew Fox ✦ *Smugglers' Cave* 169

The Authors 181

Foreword

It started over a cup of tea and scone in a restaurant in Westmoreland Street in 1996. I hadn't known of the restaurant before, which was under the street level, but Brendan did. He knows Dublin, its nooks and crannies, like the back of his hand, and the restaurant, which was like an old fashioned tea room, the kind you could find at one time in just about every town in Ireland, was near to closing time. But Brendan was well known there and we sat in a booth drinking our tea and trying not to be messy with the crumbling scones, butter and strawberry jam.

It was the wise thing to do, to go "off campus", and have the long delayed chat about an idea we both had mentioned to one another during the preceding summer, an idea that seemed on the face of it the logical thing to do. Brendan is one of the best known poets in Ireland, as well as having a distinguished record as an inspired teacher and broadcaster. He had also been involved at the very early stages of the Writers in Prisons scheme, established many years earlier with the Arts Council and Department of Justice. Over many years he had given numerous talks and readings and workshops throughout Ireland, Britain and further afield; I was trotting after him. So in a sense the idea just happened, in conversation that summer – out of the blue, off the cuff – of initiating a Masters programme in creative writing to be offered by the School of English at Trinity College Dublin, the first of its kind from an Irish university.

As we sipped our tea and thought aloud about the possibility of setting up such a course, Brendan's injunction was clear from the off: 'Keep it simple, based on individual work. *Work* shops. Small group, each year, focused on the best that they can do.' And so we set about the business of planning the ins and outs of the course, with the then head of the English department, Nicholas Grene; proposals were put in place, refined, redefined, and through the various pedagogical and methodological filters of meetings and College committees, we finally had the resources in place and key members of staff, to announce in late spring, 1997, the Master of Philosophy in Creative Writing, with Douglas Dunn, the eminent Scottish poet and professor as external examiner.

For the preceding eighteen months we had also hunted around College for a base in which to house the new programme along with the well established Masters programme in Anglo-Irish Literature, which Nicholas Grene and Terence Brown had established back in 1986. By a stroke of good fortune, after several false starts and blind alleys, we heard that the Science faculty was moving from their offices in Westland Row, and while keys to 21 Westland Row were in the gift of the TCD Oscar Wilde Society, with a little bit of effort, good will all round, and the good offices of, among others, Professor Davis Coakley, we could take over the premises, with some slight adjustments here and there so that the rooms could be used for small group teaching. Meanwhile applications for the first intake of students came flowing in. For that first term in the autumn of 1997 we met in seminar rooms in the Arts Building but by the New Year, 21 Westland Row, the house in which Oscar Wilde was born, had taken on a new life, as the Oscar Wilde Centre for Irish Writing.

Under the guidance of the then Provost, Thomas Mitchell, and more recently, John Hegarty, heads of the School of English, Nicholas Grene, Eiléan Ní Chuilleanáin, and Stephen Matterson, and, as Deans of the Faculty of Arts, John Scattergood, Eiléan Ní Chuilleanáin and Terence Brown, as well as the patronage of Merlin Holland, Oscar's grandson, the Centre took root in the life of the College, and as a metaphorical bridge between the inner world of Trinity and the hectic civic business of inner city Dublin.

The Centre sits in its own mid-19th century terrace, facing the flowing tide of commuters, the coffee shops, convenience stores, and the stream of endless traffic. Across the row the Royal Irish Academy of Music and Sweeny's Chemist, immortalized by Leopold Bloom in Joyce's *Ulysses*, Beckett's one time local, Kennedy's, and the glorious Dental Hospital of Lincoln Place, adjacent to the site of Sir William Wilde's (Oscar's father) eye and ear hospital. Nestling inside the Hamilton Building which houses the cutting edge sciences of the 21st century such as Genetics and Pharmacy, the Oscar Wilde Centre has over the past ten years been home to approximately 140 students of the creative writing programme, and over 200 students of Anglo-Irish literature. A generation of novelists, playwrights, poets, scholars, critics and teachers sharing their experience of making and reading literature in Trinity, in Dublin.

The Centre has hosted literally hundreds of guest readings, lectures, and other events over this our first ten years. The life of the house, like any family home, is now ready for the next stage of its development. Recently recognized by College as a Research Centre, plans are now in place to upgrade and refurbish the building and its facilities. But the bricks and mortar are only the outside of the Centre. What has been achieved within is what really matters. The community of students and faculty from all over the world who gather each year to study and write, young and not so young, women and men, previously published and unpublished, from all walks of life, have the chance of a year's work concentrated in one place. We have all been lucky to share in the achievements of these ten years. Students who have graduated from the M Phil in Creative Writing are now being published by leading publishers in Ireland, Britain, and elsewhere in Europe, in North America and in Australia. Others regularly see their work in print, broadcast or on stage; all are producing work of the highest literary merit.

Each year the students have the opportunity to display their work while completing their course of study in workshop, seminar and lecture. This year, 2008, sees the students of the M Phil publish in the tenth anniversary year, this splendid anthology, *Sixteen After*

Ten. To each of the sixteen involved – Carmen Cullen, Rachelle Dolan, Niall Duff, Emily Firetog, Andrew Fox, Phyl Herbert, John Holten, Viv McDade, Naoimh O'Connor, Maria Pace, Ruth Patten, Philip St John, Charlie Stadtlander, Mark Stewart, Monica Strina, Mary Turley-McGrath – heartiest congratulations from all who have been teaching on the programme this year. *Sixteen After Ten* marks an important threshold in the writing life of each of the contributors as well as in the development of the Centre. To one and to all of the very many students, teachers, guest writers, visiting fellows, external examiners, friends, supporters and partnerships of the Centre, our thanks and good wishes for the future.

Gerald Dawe

Tidal Pool

Viv McDade

FROM THE SHADOW OF THE HOUSE he watches his mother. She's barefoot and is wearing shorts and a T-shirt. A coil of hosepipe loosens behind her as she moves along the flowerbed, drenching the soil around the roots of the plants. Occasionally she bends to pull out a weed or pinch the shrivelled heads off dahlias, dropping them in a trail along the edge of the bed.

She turns back to the tap. 'Hey, Alan, you're early!'

'We all left early.' He gives her a kiss. 'The boss thinks the new programme's great.'

'That's fantastic… after all that work and worrying! We'll open some wine, drink to you tonight.' She squeezes his arm and laughs. 'How about our walk? Do you feel like it?'

'Yes, of course.'

She starts to roll up the hose and says she'll tidy things while he's changing.

Looking at himself in the mirror on his wardrobe, he thinks of duikers, the soft-eyed buck that watch from long grass, their round ears twitching. He considers himself from different angles, wonders how he might look with a beard. He loosens his tie and undresses, replacing work clothes with shorts and sandals.

In the front garden they stop to look at the lilies and she points out the ones that are opening; the white bugles and soft pink belladonnas. As they turn into the road, he looks back to the lounge window and sees the corner of the curtain drop back into place.

They stroll along the seafront, talking about little things: his work, a pair of shoes she's seen, blocks of apartments that are going up along the coast, her fiftieth birthday later that week. He teases her about a movie they'd seen at the weekend. 'Come on, Ma, you *can't* have believed all that happy-ever-after crap at the end!' A young man, his arms along the back of the bench, slides his eyes down the mother's body, then up to their faces. Alan holds his stare until he looks away.

They settle themselves on a bench close to the tidal pool. Waves roll over the edge of the pool, crawl up the beach, are hauled back into the sea. As the space between the sun and horizon closes, red and gold streaks spread across the sky. A few children run along the sand, squealing away from the reach of the waves. People shake sand from their towels, pack up cooler bags and rucksacks. A mother calls her son out of the water. He runs to her, stands with his arms around his chest while she towels his hair.

Alan watches a man sweep his arm in a wide smooth arc. He's showing two boys how to throw a Frisbee. The smaller boy grips the Frisbee and flicks his arm out from his body, shouting with frustration when it spins to the sand a few metres from his feet. Alan turns to his mother. 'It's driving him crazy that he can't do it.'

'He'll get it,' she says. 'The dad's so patient.' After a while she adds, 'Your father didn't know what to do with you once you started growing up.'

They've had this conversation before: his father's difficult boyhood, his awkwardness with people. He doesn't answer because he's thinking about the time in primary school when the teacher asked them to write a story about their fathers. The other children started writing immediately but he sat sharpening his pencil, watching the wood curl up from the blade. He could feel Miss Appel's eyes on him. He smoothed out the page, wrote down and underlined the date.

My father gave me a toy boat when I was two years old. He wrote about how his father behaved as if it was a real boat, took him down to the tidal pool, put the boat in the water right at the edge. He described how the sun felt on their backs, the shining ripples on the water, his father's gentle hands and his laughter. A strong wind came up and the boat was carried over the edge of the pool and out to sea. His father couldn't reach it and Alan cried as it sailed away.

The father knelt in the sand and put his arm around the boy. *Don't cry, son. Big boats can look after themselves on the sea.* Miss Appel gave him eight and a half out of ten and wrote at the end: *A lovely story. Well done, Alan!*

A seagull, its beak stretched wide, makes short runs along the sand, flutters up briefly, and falls back.

'Do you see it?' his mother asks. 'Something's happened to its wing.'

His mobile bleeps. It's a text from a girl at work. He smiles and keys in a response.

'It must drive you crazy, being interrupted all the time. Has she no life of her own?'

'She's OK. She's new; just trying to make friends.'

✦

It's dark by the time they get home, the little bungalow seeming to cower under the bulk of the mountain. Again the curtain moves on the lounge window. Alan leads the way to the back of the house, his mother pausing at the herb garden to break off pieces of lavender and sprigs of parsley. In the kitchen she moves pots of vegetables onto the stove and checks the oven.

'It's looking OK,' she says, 'we'll give it a bit longer.'

Alan lays a checked cloth on the Formica table, takes cutlery and the blue plates from the dresser. He sets two places at the table and puts the third plate on a metal tray with a knife and fork and a glass of water.

On the way to the bathroom he glances into the lounge. His father is in the armchair in the corner, legs stretched in front of him and ankles crossed. He's wearing khaki trousers, and the rolled sleeves of his shirt have been pushed up above his elbows. The sports section of *The Cape Times* is folded in four and he's reading with his head to one side, stroking his chin between forefinger and thumb. He raises his eyes and, without changing his expression or speaking, waits until Alan looks away.

Alan returns to the kitchen and opens a bottle of wine. His mother spoons the food onto the plates: four large potatoes for him, three for his father and one for herself. Beans and carrots and pieces of chicken. The food is positioned carefully, spillage wiped from the edges of the plates, the potatoes sprinkled with chopped parsley. A light brown gravy, thickened with Bisto and flour, is spooned over the chicken.

She carries the tray to the lounge. There's the noise of cutlery moving, sharp against the tray. At first he can't hear what's being said but his father's voice gets louder.

'He's working now, that's what I mean. It's time he got out of here.'

His mother's voice is soft and insistent. 'What's wrong with him being here? Why shouldn't he be?'

'Because I say so. That's why.' His voice is hoarse. 'It's my house. I'll say what I'll have and what I won't have.'

Alan goes to the lounge door. His mother moves in front of him.

'Go back to your dinner, Alan. Please.'

At the table they raise their glasses to each other and smile, eat in silence. Afterwards Alan washes up and they chat in low voices, his mother taking plates from the rack and drying them.

'Time for us to get out of here,' he says in a soft fierce voice.

She holds his look for a moment, gives a small shrug. 'Not now, Alan.'

In his room he boots up his computer and plays a few games before he hears footsteps into the bathroom, the toilet flushing, water trickling into the cistern. The door clicks open, the footsteps recede and another door closes.

His mother is at the kitchen table, paging through *Home and Garden* magazine. He goes in and sits opposite her. 'Aren't these blinds lovely?' she says, her slender brown fingers nervous across the page. It's difficult to tell if she is upset about what happened earlier, or if she is no longer able to care.

He wants to take her away from this place. They could move into one of the new apartment blocks farther down the coast. It's a short walk to the shops and there are movies and a bus stop close by. The ground floor apartments have little plots at the back; he would organise a truckload of compost to get the garden off to a good start. Once she had a garden, she'd feel she had a home.

'Those apartments they're building in Simonstown will be finished soon,' he says, watching her face.

'They'll be lovely. People will have fabulous views with all that glass along the front.'

'I've been thinking about buying one.'

'You planning to win the lottery?'

'Don't need to. It's only the booking fee at first. I'll have the deposit in a couple of months, get myself a mortgage. It's easy… really it is.'

She holds the edge of the table between her thumb and forefinger, chooses her words. 'No one is chasing you out of here.'

He reaches over the table, takes both her hands. 'I'm not going anywhere without you.'

'It's not that easy, Alan.'

'What's difficult about it? What do you mean?'

She doesn't answer and he feels betrayed in some way he can't understand. He shrugs to make light of it, to drop the subject. It had been a bad time to bring it up.

✦

Early on the morning of his mother's fiftieth birthday, Alan opens his window to a zinc-coloured sky and the sweet musty smell of rained-on earth. The air is still with the threat of storms. He hears the front door close and the shed open, watches his father swing himself onto his bicycle and disappear round the corner at the end of the road.

His mother is in the kitchen, making bread. She folds the dough over towards her, then pushes it away.

'Happy birthday, Ma.'

She leans forward to his kiss. 'Give me a minute here,' she says, lifting the dough into a bowl. A pot of violets is moved to one side, the bowl put on the windowsill, her hands wiped on a dishcloth.

She picks up the gift-wrapped box and is surprised it's so light. 'No shoes in here, anyway,' she laughs. She tears off the wrapping and lifts out a scroll. Her hands smooth out the paper, unrolling the pictures he's arranged: a journey down through the orchards and vineyards of the Franschoek Valley to a four-star country lodge beyond quaint village shops. It's a Cape Dutch building with high gables, ancient oaks shading the deep veranda and beds of cannas and hydrangeas bordering the lawns. The lodge is surrounded with thumbnail pictures of horse riders on mountain trails, deckchairs around a swimming pool, a terrace restaurant, a buffet of salads and meats, sauna room, beauty parlour, woven bedspreads, a sitting room with high ceilings, fireplaces and big sofas. At the bottom of the page there's a receipt for an all-inclusive weekend for two.

'Alan darling, what a beautiful, beautiful gift. But I can't let you.' She looks shy for a moment, and then laughs. 'We can't afford to go to a place like this.'

'It's my money and we can go where we like.'

She glances up at him and frowns, leans back in her chair for a moment, then folds up the wrapping paper and ribbon.

✦

He leaves work earlier than usual and stops at the market for flowers. He'd like to buy roses but poppies are her favourite. One of the sellers has buckets full of reds and pinks, oranges and whites. He tells her the flowers are for his mother's fiftieth.

'You go right on and pick out the ones you like, son,' she tells him. She takes each bloom from him, arranges the colours, is careful with the papery petals. She puts the stems into a plastic bag and wraps the whole bunch loosely in a cone of waxed brown paper.

On his way home the storm breaks: a flash of lightning followed by the crackling roar of thunder unrolling across the sky. The rain, sudden and heavy, pelts the windscreen, bounces into a milky spray on the tarmac.

He parks on the road and, shielding the flowers with his body, runs round the house and into the kitchen.

In the lounge his mother's voice is insistent. 'I didn't say it wasn't good enough. It's just not something I would wear.'

'Suit yourself then.'

'For God's sake. Things need to be chosen, tried on.'

'I wanted–' the voice wavers and stops for a moment '–to get something for you. Something for your birthday.'

He steps into the lounge. His father swings round, his face red and puffy. A dress made from soft black material with fine silver threads is crumpled on the sofa, a shoulder strap hanging over the edge. He looks at the flowers, then at Alan.

'Get the fuck out of here!'

Alan takes a step back, looks to his mother. She is standing near the window, her eyes moving anxiously between them.

His father grabs the paper cone from his hand and smashes his fist into the flowers. He twists the cone, hurls it at Alan's feet. 'Get out!' He points at the flowers, his hand trembling. 'Pick up this shit and take it with you.'

Alan bends as if he's going to pick up the flowers, then springs forward and punches his father in the mouth.

'You little fucker.' He grabs Alan by the shoulders, shoves him towards the kitchen.

'Stop it! For God's sake, stop!' screams his mother.

Everything happens in slow motion. Alan's movements are thick and clumsy; his father is like an animal panting for air. He ducks away and the older man stumbles backwards and falls, hitting his head on the coffee table.

His mother goes down on her knees, moves her husband's head

onto her lap and searches through his hair for the wound. The floor is scuffed with streaks of blood. 'Get me a cloth,' she says.

Without looking up, she takes the damp facecloth and wipes his father's head, watches the wound for a moment, then dabs it again. After a while she helps him into his chair. Alan watches her fixing a cushion behind his head, hears her say she'll make a pot of tea.

He follows her into the kitchen. She fills the kettle and puts it on the stand, looks at him for a long time, her eyes like metal. For a moment he thinks she is going to speak, but she turns away.

She pours hot water into the teapot and swirls it around twice, empties the water into the sink, drops teabags into the pot, pours water, puts two cups and a jug of milk on a tray, fills the sugar bowl and carries the tray out of the kitchen without looking back. It's like watching a stranger.

What's happening is a dream; his whole life is something he dreamed. He puts his hand to his face. The window looks as if it has been painted onto the wall, a painting of a window with darkness seeping in through the panes.

✦

He has no idea how much time has gone by. It's dark outside, the moon the shape of a cuticle, the stars fat and close. At the tidal pool, the street lamps cast a few metres of light onto the sand, but the pool itself is almost in darkness. The tide has retreated.

He bends, takes off his shoes and picks up a piece of driftwood, oval-shaped and bleached by the sun. It is smooth and comfortable in his hand and he moves it around, exploring its surface with his thumb.

His feet sink and drag until he reaches the firm wet sand. He looks back to the road. A couple passes under the streetlights, fooling about, skipping to match strides, trying to catch each other out. The girl stops, turns to the boy and laughs. They put an arm around each other and run across the road, holding out their free arms, swooping like a great bird onto the far pavement.

Everything in the tidal pool waits for the renewal the sea will bring. Hermit crabs hide in cracks. A sea star floats in a cradle of water. Tangles of yellow-brown kelp stretch along the sides of the pool, their gas-filled pods resting on the sand, waiting for the waves that will lift them to the morning sun. Alan pushes the sharp tip of a mussel shell into the driftwood, a black spread sail with grey mother-of-pearl in its curve. He wedges the little boat into a gap between the rocks and adjusts its tiny sail ready for the next cycle of the sea and an offshore wind.

Valhalla: Some Scenes in Foreign Spaces

John Holten

COWPER'S FLUID. William Day considers opening with the definition of Cowper's fluid, pre-cum, and start the interview in the worst possible way. His two interviewers sit across from him, their chairs slightly back from the desk that fills the little office. The woman is young, not much older than he is, and very attractive. The man offsets her, his bald head and forty years an extra form of grey dullness in the bland, sparse office. That such a boring space could facilitate his aroused state surprises William; he tries to divert his attention but the bare office offers little support. He has travelled far for this interview, as far north as he has ever been, and he has even enacted mock-interviews with his friends, Aug Joyce and Oliver Hamilton. Both now well-paid architects, they provided him with lots of intelligent responses to potential questions. But now the real thing is starting: the interviewers are welcoming him to Norway, thanking him for coming to the interview. He forgets his aroused state and, as always, strikes the right pose, forgets about the idea of embarrassing everyone and losing the job. He thanks them both and tells them he is delighted to be there. He is grinning madly, is sure all they are noticing is the demented rictus distorting his face.

Does he want this job or does he not?

A question from one William Day to another.

Some time later and he has started to tell himself that he does not and mentions the one thing Joyce and Hamilton told him not to: he asks about the television programme investigating the company's involvement in Guantánamo Bay, about the investigations into the company that are among the first results in a Google search for 'Aker Kværner'. He wants, out of curiosity and a forced loyalty to flippancy, to see what the response will be.

— Of course, the woman interviewer enthuses smiling brightly, of course it's only natural to want to know more about that. Put simply the programme states that Aker Kværner played a role in building part of Camp x-Ray. But if you saw the film, you would see, for example, that it does not inform you that Camp x-Ray was established in the 1990s as a facility to house nearly 30,000 boat-refugees from the Caribbean. Since 1993 Aker Kværner has carried out maintenance duties at the base, which is, don't forget, 100 years old. The TV show gives the impression that through this work, merely maintenance work, Aker Kværner has participated in violating human rights, something which is obviously a ludicrous idea and something we flatly deny. Further, we can assure you that even the company that *was* based there – it has since moved out – was the fully American-owned subsidiary Kværner Process Services Incorporated. I wouldn't worry about that at all.

It is as if she has just finished reading, the silence in the room after her speech managing to add to his despondency and his dislike of the whole role-playing routine.

— I guess that is all perfectly understandable, he says, smiling.

This is his first interview for a job as a mechanical engineer, and the alternative life he has denied himself follows him around like a bad memory. It has followed him all the way from Dublin to Oslo, through the airport, and on the train, to his hotel and out to the suburb of Fornebu and into the large office building where he sat and answered questions. He asked one or two of his own. Half-heartedly. Like a petulant child, he tried to offend his interviewers into a corner from which they would see his discomfort with the job and so refuse his application. But he betrayed his other self, the one who could have chosen another course at university, could have pursued a different career: he had asked pertinent, engaged questions about the company, showed interest, keenness. He did a good interview.

He exits the large, honeycombed Aker Hus office building and walks out under the fan-shaped atrium, continuing through the revolving doors and down the graded plaza toward the bus stop. Across the road is another large, monumental office complex: the long, low headquarters of the telephone company, Telenor. It has obviously been there facing the fjord and exposed to the north wind longer than the Aker Hus, the box hedges more mature, the gleam from the blue glass duller, the vegetation well rooted, the prospect more weary. He walks into the middle ground between the two stretched-out wings of the building and looks around him, thinking of the inevitable arrival of so many lives here every weekday morning.

On the northern wing a gigantic LED screen runs across the top of the glass façade, red words moving silently from right to left. At first, it seems like a jumble of letters and words without start or end, but soon he sees that they form sentences, phrases, aphorisms that sound like taut lines of weak poetry:

> HANDS-ON SOCIALISATION PROMOTES HAPPY INTERPERSONAL RELATIONS

> YOU ARE RESPONSIBLE FOR CONSTITUTING THE MEANING OF THINGS

He nods assent as the words silently stream by. What the hell is this? Suddenly he wakes up to the spectacle, feels little underneath it, peering up and taking in the big messages streaming forth from a source unknown for all to read.

> ELABORATION IS A FORM OF POLLUTION

EMOTIONAL RESPONSES ARE AS VALUABLE AS INTELLECTUAL RESPONSES

EXTREME SELF-CONSCIOUSNESS LEADS TO PERVERSION

Perversion. He follows the word the whole length of the board, two hundred and fifty metres at least, and sees it disappear into its silicon resting place, ready to reappear again when the time comes. Pervert – they are all a type of pervert, he thinks. This display is perverted, whatever it is or whatever its purpose. He looks around at the opaque glass sides of the waved building wondering if central management created these messages, contracting pervert psychologists to invent these aphorisms that would be full of pervert subliminal messages. He thinks of all the workers, so educated and well paid, thousands of them hidden behind the glass façades, looking out at him, at the streaming words above him and of all their dirty hidden secrets, their scurrilous kicks and fetishes. The western world over: boredom and affluence and fingers up asses.

Would he join their serried, open-planned ranks? That was, after all, what he had been preparing for all this time, all the toil and study had their end point in his settling down into the playground of work. Time to grow up.

Before he reaches the steps down to the bus stop, he turns around a final time to read one more silent message:

DISGUST IS THE APPROPRIATE RESPONSE TO MOST SITUATIONS

THEN THE NEXT DAY, one of his last days being unemployed, the home run of his student days, he walks around the Nasjonalmuseet for Samtidskunst, the city's contemporary art museum, acting like a sensitive arts student, or the poet he could have been in another voiceless reality, and there on the wall are eight white posters full of the aphorisms he had read only the day before. *Jenny Holzer* the legend card explains. This means nothing to him, but he guesses it has to be the same person behind the LED screen in Fornebu. He stands and reads every line, over two hundred trite phrases one after the other, like a savant child's punishment exercise, countless truisms written down and displayed. He turns and asks the Securitas invigilator if this artist was responsible for the large installation on the Telenor building in Fornebu.

— I don't know any Telenor building. Do they have a building in Fornebu?

He is a tall, skinny man, the same age as William.

— It doesn't matter, William replies, thanks anyway.

He turns away from the guard and makes to leave the deserted building. Ignoring the rest of the art on display, he lopes slowly through the ornate space, running his finger along the mismatched wainscotting. He has seen enough for one day.

In a sense Oslo is a city of convergence – the streets run down from the hills surrounding it and all channel themselves into the area downtown by the low entrance to the sea, as if somehow the old fort had slowly released advancing tentacles. Before reaching the fort complex, one must pass through the old, regimented streets south of Karl Johan Street, a turn or two of quadrangles, blocks of old, heavy-set buildings. It is here in these obsidian blocks, buildings reminiscent of Manhattan or some such metropolis, that William has secured a hotel. He instantly liked it: away from the commercial chatter of Karl Johan, the relatively quiet, austere density of the intersecting blocks appealed to him. Few people live there – the buildings too old to handle the attendant sewage – and commerce is sporadic. There are offices and some brown pubs, as the locals call the sparsely decorated, cheap bars, some cultural sites, sex shops and prostitutes who skulk along the footpaths, lending the district the final veneer of a rough-edged downtown harbour borough. Now, as he makes his way into the area, his phone rings and quite simply he is offered the job and he accepts it. He is now employed; he is in the playground of salaried adults.

He sits at the gate, waiting to board, and thinks of Aug Joyce and

Oliver Hamilton, their excitement at words such as 'non-place' and 'supermodernity', Zaha Hadid and Frank Gehry – all the glib soundbites from their learning which he recalls them rattling off between lectures. All as empty and detached from reality as Jenny Holzer's phrases, stuck up on the wall of a museum for art students and obedient tourists to laugh in front of. Now he is sitting in the airport, saying to himself that it is just an airport, a *non-place* between arriving and departing, like thousands of other airports, and that now he has this job he will be passing through many of them. And he tells himself that these airport spaces will be real to him. They will be moments in his working life. He assures himself that on the internet he can go to those non-places maybe, click on a scroll bar and say to himself Ciampino is not Rome, Paris is not Beauvais, Stansted is not London and Girona is not Barcelona. But he realises as he stands up and gets into the queue that such an act would be immature, ironic and facile, something that is behind him. Ciampino is Ciampino, Beauvais is Beauvais, Torp is Torp: and you get what you pay for. Decisions made are decisions to defend in the real world, he tells himself as he hands over his boarding card and passport. And he is happy that this is the world and that he can recognise it.

THE ANTEROOM IS DRAB, BARE, a space for passing through, nothing more. Older men well used to the routine sit hunched and surprisingly attentive to the safety video. It plays out a nightmare of a helicopter crash out over the sea: the escape, the survival, life rafts and removing helicopter windows at high speed. He watches it and tells himself it is all routine, just part of the job. He is in his immersion suit ready for the threat of a cold sea swim, earplugs shutting off outside noise, leaving him with the drumming of his own overly excited heart.

He is flying out in the same pioneering spirit as countless people have done before him. He is in the search for the last of the North Sea oil. He has a big salary and he has to go to places far and wide. His expertise is needed and his enthusiasm welcome.

He is out on the tarmac of the heliport, air pounding him from all sides. The machine is dull, old-looking. For almost four hours it fights the cloud, ratcheting itself windward, the black sea gushing below. After nearly two hours the intercom comes on and he is warned that the weather at the rig is not so good: they might be turning back. Then suddenly the clouds part and he opens his eyes, sees the tiny coin of the helipad surrounded by the dirt-black heaving sea.

As the wall of wind hits him, almost flattening him, his squint eyes registering the lack of a parapet on the tiny landing space, the waves foaming and surging just fifty feet below him, he tells himself how he got to be there: the breath of coincidence and sad events, endless repetitions of someone else's life story, some unfortunate stranger. Moving unsteadily down the metal mesh steps which float above the abysmal, roiling sea below, he tells himself he is that stranger. He enters through a rust-encrusted door, bows his head and moves down the low corridor, the warm air buffeting his immersion suit. It is like outer space or something less glamorous – a building-site at sea, a demented experiment in survival. He is the stranger trying to survive.

The same stranger who had fluid in his pants, who gave his interviewers a charming smile.

The very one who read twice in two days the *Truisms* of the artist Jenny Holzer, and in different locations across a city he had never been to before.

He is the same William Day only he is abroad in a world with a Guantánamo Bay in which he has no need to feel complicit.

He is the one who was offered the job and he is the one who took it.

— William Day? Welcome to the Valhall-Amoco Platform.

What We Remember in Forgetting

Emily Firetog

WE ALLOWED GEORGE TO DRINK because Derek's mom had once told Derek that it could help with the Alzheimer's, but we had to watch him because he was sneaky and got himself another drink without anyone really noticing, and then in the middle of saying something about the piano he just put his head down on the table and fell asleep. It was hell trying to wake him up to take his evening medication.

Derek's mom told me she needed a vacation – just a little time off, that's all. It had been hard on her: George was stage two at least, though no one was sure, and Derek was off at school. She wanted to go to Chicago to see her sister for a couple of days, a week at the most. There was a nurse that could take care of him, their insurance would pay for it, but she came to ask me first – I needed the money, I always needed the money – and she would fill out the forms and I could get $800 for the week. Of course I would do it, I said; George was like a father to me.

It was good to get away from my apartment too, because ever since my girlfriend Jackie moved in she hadn't left the apartment, except to go to work, and even then she had started taking fewer shifts. I would come home and she would be sitting with an empty peanut butter jar on the couch and would start crying and then I could hear her go throw up in the bathroom. It was good to get away because I didn't know what to do about that.

I got to Derek's house early and his mom was packing up her car. George was sitting on the porch smoking a cigarette.

'Hey Neil,' Derek's mom said, kissing my cheek.

'Hi.' Derek's mom was a poet. She had published a small book – vanity press. It was reviewed in the local paper and she even gave a reading at the local library and at the college up the road. If she got famous, they could become a family of famous artists. But George was just starting to get bad, and then when he was diagnosed she didn't worry too much about publishing any more.

'George, you remember Neil, Derek's friend?'

George nodded, but I wasn't really sure if he remembered me.

'Remember I said Neil's going to stay here while I visit my sister Loddie in Chicago?'

'Yep,' George said.

'He's not great today, a little tired I think.' We walked inside and Derek's mom showed me where all the medication was, which toothbrush was George's, where his clothes were. In their bedroom were three shelves of books – the first was all poetry and anthologies of poetry, the second was about music and Italy, the last was overflowing and there was even a small pile next to it on the floor. They had titles like 'Caring for Loved Ones with Alzheimer's.' Derek's mom saw me looking and nudged the pile with her foot.

'These are the latest addition to our library, obviously,' she said sighing. 'They don't tell you anything, but you can read them if you get bored.'

Growing up you know where your friends live and you see your friends' bedrooms. You can find where their moms keep the snacks and what's in their refrigerator, but you don't see your friends' parents' bedrooms, their underwear drawers. You might see where they keep a dirty magazine, but only if your friend found it first. The bedrooms of your friends' parents are more secret than your own parents' bedrooms, even if your parents lock the door at night and your dad would smack you across the face if he ever caught you snooping in his drawers.

'He's already eaten breakfast,' Derek's mom said, moving back through the living room and leaning against the open front door. George was still outside smoking. 'And don't let him have too many cigarettes,' she said, kissing my cheek again. 'Thanks, Neil.'

When my mother died, Derek's mom came over a couple times and cooked dinner with me. She was fifty-five – breast cancer – but the medication made her so thin, so yellow and dry, that when she died she looked almost eighty. Derek's mom helped me pack up the house since it didn't make any sense staying there by myself. When we were filling boxes, she found a load of pictures of Derek and me all the way back in kindergarten and I let her take a bunch. We were sitting on the floor of my living room.

'Do you remember this? We took you guys to the Montpellier Zoo?' she said, laying the photographs out on the floor in a grid.

'I remember, but only from the pictures, I guess. My mom would always tell me the story about a petting zoo – was that there?'

'Yes, yes there was a petting zoo. All you and Derek wanted to do was pet the animals, but when we finally got you there both of you were terrified and had to be carried. George nearly threw out his back because you wanted to be held together.'

'And when we left, I asked when we were going to go back?'

'I thought it was Derek, but it might have been you. I can't remember,' she said, patting my hand.

It was around when my mom died that George was first diagnosed. He was only fifty years old. Early Onset Alzheimer's.

As we put the photographs away, Derek's mom said absently, 'I don't know what to expect. Maybe it would be better if he just died before it all went away.' I didn't say anything then, but I remembered it. I wondered if she still thought like that, or if she could admit she had ever felt like that, now that it really had all gone away.

I walked outside and leaned against the porch railing and watched George, who had finished his cigarette and was watching nothing. A black car went down the road and his eyes didn't follow it.

We were sitting on the couch watching a soccer game on television when the doorbell rang. I went to the door and opened it and Derek was standing there with a big green suitcase and a beard, which I had never seen him have before. His eyebrows were up and mouth agape like he had just been secretly punched in the kidneys.

'Jesus fucking Christ, Neil! What are you doing here?'

'I'm looking after your dad. Your mom's visiting her sister for the week.'

'For the week?'

'Yeah.'

'Man, how are you?' he said, dropping his bag. He gave me a big hug.

'Getting along.' I looked at my shoes.

'Can I come in?'

'Yeah, of course, man; it's your house. Your dad's in the living room watching a game.'

We walked in and Derek put his bag on the couch.

George stood up and looked towards us.

'Hey Dad,' he said, walking over to him, 'It's Derek.'

'He knows who you are,' I said.

'I mean, it's been a while.'

'The beard,' George said. 'It's new.'

'Do you like it?' Derek asked, running his hands over and through it like he was stroking a pet.

'Not really,' George said.

We laughed.

'I was going to make some lunch,' I said. 'George, do you want lunch?'

'Yeah,' he said.

I went into the kitchen to make some omelets and let Derek talk to his dad in the living room. After a couple of minutes I heard the sound on the game get turned up and Derek came into the kitchen.

'So my mom's gone?' he asked, opening the refrigerator. He bent down to the back of the bottom shelf and pulled out the orange juice container. He drank straight from the box.

'I told you, she's visiting your aunt in Chicago. You didn't call first?'

'What's with the third degree? I thought I could come home for a while – see you. It's been a while, man.'

'A couple of months, yeah.'

Derek sat down at the kitchen table and took a plate of eggs and a slice of bread from the toaster. He had a few bites, nodding in thanks. I made another plate and brought it out to George with a glass of water and then came back in.

'Why are you watching him? I thought he had a nurse.'

'Sometimes. But your mom asked me to watch him. She worked out something so I could get paid. Every little bit helps, you know?'

'Are you qualified?' he asked, raising his head. It wasn't a challenge; he was concerned. He just didn't know how to express it.

'Your mom explained everything to me. There's a lot of medication, that's all. I took care of my mom, you know, when she got sick. I'm used to it.'

Derek went back to his eggs and I ate my share standing over the oven, straight from the frying pan.

I walked back out into the living room and sat down next to George, who had his empty plate on his lap.

'Were the eggs good?' I asked.

'Yeah,' he said.

The soccer game had ended and now there was a golf tournament on. There were aerial shots of large green fairways and trees; it was sunny wherever they were playing. If I took a vacation, that's the sort of vacation I'd want – the kind that I would need. Silence, green, trees. Not a city like Chicago, wind and smoke and more people. Then, it's the silence that's probably getting to Derek's mom; it's the noise of the city that will do her good.

'Smoke?' George asked.

'Yeah, let's go outside,' I said. I took two cigarettes out of George's pack and we went out to the front porch. George was having trouble with the lighter, so I helped him. We sat on the porch swing but didn't swing. There was a couple walking down the street with a baby carriage. The man was older, balding. He was wearing a vest and dress shoes that clicked on the sidewalk. The woman had her hair tucked up under her hat; she almost looked bald too. Every few feet she would stop the man from pushing the carriage and bend down and say something to her baby, adjust the blanket, rearrange the baby toys inside. Then she would stand, look up, and smile.

I finished my cigarette and went inside to call Jackie.

'I'll be right back, George,' I said. 'I'm just going in the house for a minute. Should I tell Derek to come out?'

'OK,' he said.

Derek wasn't in the living room and I figured he was unpacking his stuff. I went to the phone and called home. There was no answer. I left a message on our answering machine: 'Jackie, it's me. Just checking in. George is fine. Derek's back, actually. He just showed up a couple hours ago. Hope everything's OK. I'll call you later tonight.'

Derek walked down the stairs as I was hanging up.

'My mom?' he asked.

'No. Jackie. She wasn't in.'

'You guys still together?'

'Yeah,' I said. We went outside.

'I need to pick up some booze,' Derek said, swinging his car keys.

'A party?'

'Just us, to celebrate my return.'

'George, do you want to go for a car ride? Do you want to go get some beer?' I asked.

'Sure,' he said.

So we piled into the car to go on a liquor run. It was almost like high school again, Derek driving us around in his old Honda, which was now ancient – the same except George was in the backseat.

'George, you have your seatbelt on?' I asked. I heard the belt click.

We took the same route we used to, the same left turn and back road so that we wouldn't pass my house and no one could see us until we turned onto Hanover Road, right into the Liquor Mart's parking lot.

'What do you want to listen to?' I asked George.

'I don't know,' he said, looking out the window.

'How about some rock and roll?' I asked.

'OK.'

'I can't figure out how to talk to him,' Derek said, making the turn.

'You just talk normal,' I said. I fiddled with the radio dial until we got to the rock station and leaned back in the seat and closed my eyes. 'Just explain everything you're doing. Narrate your life.'

'This station still exists?' Derek said. '92.5 FM, Barre's only r-r-r-r-r-ock station!'

'There are a lot of rock stations in New York?'

'I mean, of course, but I don't listen to the radio that much. I'm working a lot.'

'Making art?'

'In school we're working with plastics, sculpting and building – it's very innovative, I think, but there's a lot of directed creativity. That's why I'm home now. You know? I need some space to develop on my own.'

'You left school? You left New York to come back here?'

'You wouldn't understand, I guess.'

We didn't say anything else until we pulled up to the Liquor Mart and got out of the car. I opened George's door and he got out.

'We're going to get some beer,' I said to him as we walked in the store. 'Do you want beer?'

'Yeah,' he said.

In the store George and I walked to the coolers in the back and picked out two six-packs. Derek got his own stuff and we met up at the counter. George walked in front of us and started stuttering to the man at the counter. I was going through my wallet looking for my debit card and wasn't paying attention. George leaned forward and stuttered more; he was pointing at a spot on the counter and tapping it, looking at it. The cashier was my age and was shaking his head. He had his hands clenched, like he was scared of George.

'I'm sorry, what do you want?' he said.

'Neil,' Derek said. 'Help him.'

'What?' I looked up and saw it, saw George pointing and tapping. He couldn't think of the word he needed, or if he had it, it wouldn't come out. It danced on his tongue, in the back of his throat, frozen.

'George you want something there?' I asked. He looked at me like he was looking through me. 'You want a lotto ticket,' I said, looking at the wall behind the cashier. 'Cigarettes?'

'Yes,' he said.

'George, you already have cigarettes. We bought a new pack yesterday. I have them right here. You want one?'

He nodded and we went outside. Derek stayed inside and paid for everything and then met us with two small paper bags. We walked to the car and George leaned against the trunk and finished his cigarette. Looking at him you wouldn't know anything. You wouldn't suspect. Derek got in the car and waited. We drove home and didn't say anything. We didn't even turn on the radio.

Derek and I had had two beers each and left the rest of the pack in the kitchen. George went to the bathroom and when he came back he had opened another beer and was drinking it.

'Dad, you have one right here. You didn't finish this one yet,' Derek said.

That's when we had to start watching him because then he finished two beers, and there was another half-drunk can in the kitchen that might have been his too.

'Do you know if he still plays?' I asked.

'He did when it first started, but not any more,' Derek said.

'The piano?' George asked.

'Yeah Dad, the piano. Do you still want to play the piano? Do you miss it? Do you want to play it now?'

He paused and looked down at the table and at his hands, which were spread out flat on the tablecloth.

'I don't know,' he said. Then his head went down and I had to get him up to take his meds.

'Tired George? Want to go to sleep?' I asked.

He nodded, sleepily. A giant child, a graying baby.

I watched George swallow his pills in the bathroom; he'd put one in his mouth and then I'd hand him the glass of water and we'd do this five or six times, back and forth. I stood outside and looked at my nails while he brushed his teeth and then we went into his bedroom and I handed him a shirt from the drawer Derek's mom had showed me.

'You have to change for bed now, George,' I said.

He took off his shirt. His chest was still tanned brownish from the summer; he had a thin line of white hairs from his throat to his belly button. I was sitting on the bed of Derek's parents' room watching his father change his shirt.

'Do you remember who played in the soccer game this afternoon?' I asked. 'The one we watched on television before Derek rang the doorbell?'

He shook his head.

'It's OK, I don't remember either. But then we went in the car to get some beer and pizza, remember? We drank some beer and ate the pizza just now.'

'Yep, pizza and beer.'

I gave George clean underwear and told him I was going to go into the living room with Derek and he should go to sleep but if he needed anything he should just come out into the hall.

'Thank you.'

'Goodnight, George.'

'Ok, goodnight.'

In the living room Derek was lying down on the couch looking up at nothing but his eyes were going back and forth, side to side like one of those cat clocks in old cartoons.

'You OK?' I asked.

'I was just waiting for you to come back.'

'Your dad's asleep.'

'You want to drink some more?' He held up a new bottle of something he must have picked up at the Liquor Mart.

'Sure.'

Derek rolled off the couch and sat down on the floor with his knees up and hung his head in between. I sat down across from him, leaning on the ottoman, and reached over for the bottle.

'Have you sold any art?' I asked.

'No,' he said. 'No one sells art any more.'

'Oh.'

We drank some more.

'Jackie?' he asked.

'I don't know. It's complicated.' I didn't want to say anything else.

Derek took another sip from the bottle and rolled the cap back and forth between his fingers. He had dripped some of the liquor onto his beard. He ran his hands across it a couple of times, but I couldn't tell if he was wiping it off or just playing with it, like he'd been doing all day.

'I appreciate you looking after him and all,' Derek said. 'I don't know how to deal with it.'

'You should spend some time with him. He wasn't really talkative today, but sometimes he's better.'

Derek crawled over to the bookcase across from us.

'When was the last time you listened to him?' he asked. 'Have you listened to him since you've been here?'

'No. It's been years actually. Maybe when he first, you know, I played some of it.'

Derek nodded and looked through the records on the bottom shelf of the bookcase. He took out a record and put it on the turntable next to the television. I held my breath during the airy silence before it started, that white noise of oncoming tension. George had been an avant-garde composer – *the* innovator of the twelve-note symphony. It began quickly. We closed our eyes and listened to the cacophony of staccato sound; soft and a-melodious.

'I don't understand it,' Derek said finally.

'I don't either.'

'Is it beautiful? Is it supposed to be?'

'No, I don't think so.'

We lay down on the carpet and looked up at the ceiling. Faintly, I could hear George snoring in his bedroom. The music got louder.

A pattern developed that I tried to follow. I had it, I saw it, and then it slipped away, becoming something else. I couldn't imagine George sitting at the piano, in a recording studio, in a concert hall. When we were kids, he had traveled a lot. He inspired an entire movement in Italy. I felt like I was spinning now – the liquor, suddenly, had made me drunk. I realized that next to me Derek was breathing hard, maybe crying, and I tried to reach my hand out to him but couldn't tell where he was next to me. His breathing was harder and I was sure he was crying now but I couldn't turn my head to look at him.

Poems

Mary Turley-McGrath

Knockanare

It took less than a week to skin the sods
from the sloping acres of O'Donnell's field.

By late summer the green had bled to reddish-brown,
the top-soil heaped in pyramids at the lowest end.

This morning's crow-call over Knockanare loosens
layers of my fading sleep, draws me back to world time.

I reach the roadside as machines rev up,
see the last fifty yards of ditch: hawthorn, ash, rosehip,

split roots jutting from flattened earth
like lengths of broken bones.

Dreamwood

This time of year
in the fretwork of skewed seasons
I think of you;

trees are touched with green,
road edges banked with hailstones
like saltpetre.

Your canvas stretches on the frame,
the purple one you cut back
and repainted blue and green,
with long turquoise brushstrokes;
the rim of purple remained
like a ripened bruise.

What if the vernal matrix breaks,
 the calends fail, the seasons poison,
 or the Arctic ice thaws, while you
 paint in your house above the sea?

Will I find in your scheme
 the patinas of the dreamwood
 we will visit at the end of May?

The Silence

He grew up by the sea.
There were fishing boats and forests.
All day the sawmills whined,
preparing trees for the town
down the river.

He feared the next pogrom:
his family herded into the synagogue,
doors nailed up,
straw roof set ablaze,
screams carrying north into the cool Nordic air,
to the fjords he visited one lovely summer as a child.

He wished they had stayed in the long narrow channels
of deep blue water.

At last, he gathered their possessions;
stacked everything on one small cart,
took a train from the town and sailed
to the hubbub of an English city.

Rathlin

The moon over Rathlin
scans the Sea of Moyle
that licks the rocks
below the road at the end
of the pebble-covered garden.

Moonlight selects the waves,
pulses of dark and light –
turns them to a phalanx of soldiers
carrying black spears, racing
to hide in the rocks.

The clouds heave away
towards the West Lighthouse;
the sky becomes the shimmering
abalone shell I gave you
when we stayed in your house

near the Black Castle. We slept
that night to the sea's deep moan,
so that I felt I had been borrowed
by the sea and returned home
with the morning sun.

Museo Picasso Málaga

It is late afternoon when we leave
the white rooms with their spotlights
blended to the point of natural light.
Everything in white and black, except
the paintings of deconstructed bodies
reassembled in geometric overlaps;
no tenderness between objects
and humans or in the reclining nudes.

The air is cool outside. Poinsettias
stacked in high circular stands warm
the eye. A young couple lounge
in wicker chairs outside the café, smile
at two black kittens playing on the steps
of San Agustín. They drink cappuccinos,
gaze into each other's eyes, unaware
of the churchgoers making their way
up the steps for evening prayer.

At the Cathedral the orange trees
are laden with fruit. Christmas lights,
laced through branches, flicker,
the oranges momentarily come alive.
The black seats under the trees are empty;
no tired tourists finding rest and shade,
no flower-sellers with armfuls of carnations
seeking payment in cent from the purse
while robbing euro from the pocket.

In Café El Jardín, the aroma of coffee
floats around six cast-iron columns
and the canopy over the bar,
decorated with gold stuccowork.
Tendrils pour from skylight plants;
plaster-casts of poets and writers
look down from above the tables;
names I do not know: Rubio Arguilles,
Ángel Cafferena, Salvador Rueda.

Rachel in the Garden

I wait for her on the narrow path
between towering artichokes.
One has flowered,
a huge purple-blue, big as my fist,
a giant's signet ring to taunt
the grey clouds moving west.

She arrives.
We move along the gravel path,
pull weeds here and there, leave
the bunch of scarlet poppies.
Once I kept this clear, she said,
but now I cannot bear
to pluck wild poppy flowers.

We talk about the Wars,
our connections with them:
how in west Donegal
the poppy and the shamrock
are worn together;
how her father saved
the photograph of a German soldier
she hid in a book and cannot find,
but looks for still.

Down the steps she names for me
viburnum, alchemilla mollis, astilbe.
The two-hundred-year-old redwood
at the corner of the lawn.
We look across the lake at chestnut,
willow, ash and elder.
There is a longing
for autumn's colours in her voice.

The Smoking Car

Charlie Stadtlander

Gliding east across the North Dakotan prairie on the Empire Builder passenger rail line, I sat across from three young Muslim women in the observation car. They wore well-tailored black dresses that ran from neck to ankle, insisting on modesty but nonetheless hinting at their eye-catching curves in the journey south. They shrouded their heads in loosely falling white cloths and veiled their mouths with delicate panes of lace. Only their neat noses, smoky eyes, and eyebrows – rich, dark, and full – remained completely visible.

As they spoke in soft voices to each other, I found it difficult to distinguish exactly who was talking. This communication approached a form of ESP, as I imagine a future race of people will one day converse – facing each other and transmitting thoughts without interference from the weaknesses of the human mouth and tongue.

I ambled towards them, lifted my hat and lowered my glasses, removing all barriers I had control of, and said with no general specificity, 'Hello, how do you do? Lovely ride we're having isn't it? Allow me to introduce myself.'

The one with the oldest-looking eyes raised her hand, as if aware of my inability to tell them apart. 'Hello. I will allow you to do so, but I cannot promise we will be as forthcoming in our replies.'

'Well, hmm. OK. In any case, my name is Wallace Pound. I'm on my way home to Chicago from a business trip in Portland. What brings you onto the train? Visiting family?'

'Yes,' said the second of the three, not the one who had just spoken. 'We have family we're going to see. We prefer not to fly if at all possible.'

'Ah yes.' I saw a crack in which to drive a conversational wedge. 'Hardly anybody takes the train these days, what with the airlines and all. It's just a relic of a bygone time, I suppose. Me? I like taking the train, as long as I can spare the time. There's too much of a hurry these days, don't you think? The two days on the train give me a chance to read a couple books, meet interesting strangers such as you ladies, and enjoy the breathtaking scenery of the Northern Plains. Isn't it lovely?'

Another of them spoke, though at first I wasn't sure if it was number three or two, for both talked in equally soothing, girlish voices, completely unaccented. 'Yes, I do not disagree – the views from the observation car are quite picturesque. And, actually, we are in a hurry. There is a wedding tomorrow evening.' It was the third one speaking. 'When we arrive in Chicago in the morning, we must rush to prepare for the ceremony that afternoon. Train travel does have its benefits, though. The three of us get to enjoy the comfort and privacy of a sleeping compartment. And lately,' she paused, her dusky eyelids closing themselves gently for a moment, 'women dressed like *us* cannot always board airplanes without incident, if you understand what I mean.'

'Ah, I think I do. Terrible times we live in, if you ask me. Just because someone has a beard, a turban, or a, a...what do you call what you're wearing?'

'A *burkha*.'

'Right, or a burkha. That doesn't mean they should be automatically suspected of having dynamite taped to their torso. I mean, in my opinion, there are lots of people who blow things up who aren't Muslim, and there are even more Muslims who'll never blow anything up in their lives, or even think of doing it. Not that many people of any religion ever consider exploding things, buildings or cars – you know what I mean?'

The oldest of the three spoke again. 'Well, thank you, I suppose. That isn't an opinion we encounter very often. Perhaps if more people in America thought like you, we could walk on to planes with fewer second looks from the staff and fellow passengers. Until then, we are content to take the train and enjoy the scenery, just like you. It's rare that we can go to public places like airports without getting constant stares from ignorant people the whole time. It's like the opposite of a person with a massive burn scar or dwarfism. For them, adults know better than to stare and judge, and only the children drop their jaws and point. For us, however, the children are the ones wise and innocent enough not to suspect anything, and the foolish adults are left trading whispers with each other and looking at the three of us like we were pariahs.'

'Gosh, that must be a constant struggle.' I smiled at her. I thought I saw the lace over her mouth budge. 'I feel terrible for your situation, but I'm glad you three were forced to take the train today, or I wouldn't have had the pleasure of meeting you.'

The three of them lowered their heads in unison, and one of them said 'Thank you, we appreciate your kindness.' They resumed gazing out of the swiftly moving train. The observation car was lined with tall windows that curved over the ceiling, providing perhaps thirty more degrees of visibility. As silence fell over the four of us, we all sighed in mutual appreciation of the way the vast blue sky met the tawny earth, dotted periodically with pale green sagebrush.

'Now, I'm not saying I agree with the people on the planes, but what if you just didn't wear your burkta–'

'*Burkha.*'

'Right, sorry. What if you didn't wear them when you flew? Just to make the whole process go a bit more, eh, swimmingly, you know?'

The three of them turned their gaze from the windows to me. The oldest of the three took charge again. 'Do you know what you're talking about? How dare you suggest such a thing! To do that would be to yield to racism and prejudice, to erase who we are as people, as women, and to deface our history and family.'

'No, I didn't mean it like that. I was just saying that their prejudices will always be what they are, wrong as they may be, so wouldn't it be easier for you–'

'Please, just stop now. Life and love of God isn't about making things easy. You are just as ignorant as anyone we've encountered. Leave us be.'

I did. I slunk away without reply, towards the back of the observation car, near where it meets the smoking car. The best place to pass the hours on a train – truly make them fly – is always in the smoking car, at the rear of the train. It lies away from the families that sprawl across too many seats. It's also far more elite and sophisticated than the awkward dining car, where the train staff, in the name of efficiency, fill up tables with separate groups of people. *Party of two, party of three, party of one, you are now party of six.* And most importantly, the smoking car is a more pleasant environment than any dreadful observation car. It affords almost the same panorama (no wrap-around windows), but with none of the aimless and overly polite conversation.

Smokers are a group chosen by each other, all aware and appreciative of our common purpose of escape and indulgence. More importantly, smoking is a perfect companion to conversation. The controlled inhalation and exhalation of smoke has an innate ability to build and release drama at critical moments of a story. The glowing coal of a cigarette serves as a visual punctuation to sentences, a conductor's baton for the speaker. Nicotine is the perfectly dosed stimulant – enough to get your mind whirring and to let the words unroll invitingly, keeping your audience rapt, but not too much of an upper to spin your wheels past the limit. But most importantly, we smokers are in charge of our own mortality, so there's no tap-dancing around requisite niceties and protocol of conversation for conversation's sake. We're all there to do one thing. Using that as a starting point, it's easy to move forward. Nobody would misunderstand me here.

I slid the door dividing the cars shut behind me, reached into the breast pocket of my blazer, took out a cigarette from the pack, and lit it in one fluid motion. I collapsed onto the bench seat and looked back through the window into the observation car. The three women convened their veiled heads, trading more of their hushed words. I saw one of them crane her neck to look at me and lightly shake her head in disapproval.

Just as I took a soothing inhalation, I felt a timid nudge to my ribcage. I looked to my right and found myself eye to eye with a youngish Middle Eastern man, about my age, with a weak attempt at a moustache under his nose. A thin cigarette, neatly wrapped in a green leaf, drooped from his lips.

'I see you were talking to my three sisters over there. Were you trying to pick one of them up or something? Did you think you could talk one of them into ducking into your sleeper compartment for a quick toss around? What the hell were you doing?'

I stammered for a moment, searching for what could possibly explain my trespass against what must have been some sort of generations-old Islamic family protection rule. The man stared at me viciously for another few seconds. He pinched the little imported cigarette and held it in front of his face, as if he was aiming a dart.

'So, what do you have to say for yourself, huh? Go on, explain!' His face started to twitch, and with a snort, a large puff of smoke plumed from his nose. 'Hoo! I had you there for a second, didn't I?' He clapped my shoulder. 'Don't worry about my sisters. My dad expects me to watch after them just because I'm the man of the four siblings, but who really cares? They're older than I am, anyway. I don't know what he expects me to do. Besides, if you had one sister sitting alone over there, let alone three, you'd have to be watching me *pretty* closely. Don't sweat it, man.'

'Really? You did get me, I gotta admit. Thanks for joking about it though, I feel pretty lousy right now. I think I might have actually said something to offend them.'

He dragged before he spoke, letting a bit of the smoke pop out with each word. 'Oh man, was it about their burkhas? They get really sensitive about that, and for no good reason! They don't even have to wear those things. I mean, women in the country we come from don't even wear the ones with face coverings. I think they're just doing that to impress our parents, so they'll like them better than me. They're like born-again Muslims or something. I don't know what.'

'Where does your family come from anyway, if you don't mind me asking?'

'Nah, it's OK. My parents are Persian, but we were all born in America.'

'Persian, hmm?' I searched the blurry world atlas in my head for where Persia lay on a map. Was it in Northern Africa? Next to Israel? Nearer to India?

'Yeah, but that doesn't really mean anything now. Persia is just a nice way of saying Iran. Technically, there hasn't been such a thing as a Persian in decades, but when we move to America, we don't want to tell people we're Iranians. *Persian* just rolls off the tongue a bit better, don't you think? My name's Darius, by the way.'

I lipped my own cigarette and shoved a hand out towards him. 'Wally Pound, Darius. Pleased to meetcha. Put 'er there.' We shook our clasped hands vigorously. 'So, before I pissed them off, your sisters said you were on the way to a wedding.'

'Yeah, that's right. Some cousin that I've only met once, many years ago. I'm not really looking forward to it. Weddings are events for women anyway, don't you think? At best, maybe I can meet a hot friend of some relative there. But with those three lurking around, I'll have a more difficult time of that. Plus, I have to give some sort of a speech there about the solemn joy of the day – another unfortunate holdover of tradition.' He squinted his eyes at his sisters and mimed throwing his dart in their direction.

'Ugh, I know what you mean. My brother got married last year, and I had to give a best man's speech. He's my goddamned *brother*, and I still didn't even know what to say. I know what you'll be up against. It'll just be a lot worse for you.'

'Well, if you don't mind, I can try out what I'm going to say. You can give a listen, let me know what sense it makes to you.'

I agreed heartily. It was perfect smoking car pastime fodder, and with about twenty hours until we got to Chicago, it's not like I didn't have the time to spare. I lit a fresh cigarette, placed another behind my ear for easy access, and bathed in the exhaled blue smoke as Darius began talking.

'Right, so this takes place when there were *proper* Persians, over a thousand years ago in the days of Emperors and tribes. A young family belonged to one of these tribes, in a desolate village nestled among the foothills of the mighty Hindu Kush Mountains. The village had a long-practiced tradition of burning the clothes and belongings of relatives after they died. The belief was that the material possessions contained the ill spirits of death within them, and the dead are best and most fondly remembered when these foul feelings are exterminated.

'The family in the story was faced with a tough decision. They were quite poor, and a rich and cruel aunt of theirs died alone at an old age. The time had come for the family to burn all her things. However, her death came just as the last warmth of summer ran away from the cold peaks of the Hindu Kush. Autumn was passing quickly and the wind-driven snow of winter was only weeks away. Among the dead old woman's things were chests full of rare and costly animal furs – enough to keep the young married couple and their two young children warm through the winter. They secretly kept these important clothes and ceremoniously burned some useless possessions of the aunt in front of the village, to show their allegiance for tradition and to give the impression that the specters of death were leaving the village.

'Each night when the children of the family wore the furs, they could feel the evil memories of the woman present in the house, and it scared them awake. Eventually, after several nights of fear-filled sleeplessness, the children of the house were huddled together in the dark, and the youngest called out to the memories themselves – *leave us, nobody wants you here!* This outcry, strangely, seemed to put a stop to the presence of the awful feelings. In the following nights, if even a hint of the ill spirits returned to the house, the children would glare angrily into the dark and firmly assert that nobody was scared, and the memories were just wasting their time trying to haunt this house.

'Contrary to what the village believed, simply speaking with the dead was entirely possible. When the ice of winter thawed, the family showed everyone in the village the furs they had used to survive. They related the tale of how they had yelled the aunt's memory out of their lives. *All those wasted clothes in our history*, everyone said.

'I guess in those days, few things were more valuable than clothes. The villagers realized they could have been facing their bad memories and shutting them out all along. And so they started a new ritual: Shouting at the Dead. Funerals became all-night sessions of accusatory screaming at the departed, instead of solemn ceremonies of mourning followed by wasteful bonfires.'

When Darius finished talking, his cigarette had burned down almost to his lips. He plucked it from his mouth and stubbed it out in the aluminum ashtray sunken in the armrest. He looked away from me, out the window at the scrolling landscape as the last remnants of his cigarette smoke seeped from his nostrils. 'What does that story mean to you?'

'Fur is murder?'

He laughed and shook his head. 'Are you ever serious? Honestly, what do you think it means?'

I paused and really tried to think about it. 'I guess it means that, as a people, there's no reason for us to blindly follow wrong traditions of the past, just because we're told that we're supposed to. Customary doesn't always mean correct, right?'

'That's a very American answer, and I like where you're coming from, but unfortunately it's a misinterpretation of the folk tale. This whole country was started on the premise of flipping off England – even though England deserved it, both from us and from all their colonies around the world. But, ever since then, Americans have been proud of taking apart authority, restriction, and history, brick by brick. There is more to learning than a clean sweep. No, the point of the story is that traditions *are* correct. Either way, burning or yelling, the people needed to be free of the haunted memories of the dead. For centuries before, the burning *worked*. The revelation by the small child of the family was merely an evolution in technology, improving the process of performing the same task.'

I thought about this for a few seconds as our clouds of smoke lazily floated through the train car. After a moment, I said 'So when you tell this story at a wedding, it instructs the newlywed couple to live their new lives fresh and excitingly, but also to be aware of the love and work of all other married couples before them which have brought them to this point?'

'Yes, exactly. Sort of. It's a Persian thing, and I'm not sure I completely understand it myself. I guess I liked it because every other folk tale I came across was rooted in predictable Islamic parable. This one just had something *bigger* about it, something universal that I think people everywhere can learn something from. Hopefully this cousin and his new wife can find something in it, kind of like I did. And even if they don't, it'll be another fifteen years before I see these people again, so who cares?

'I guess in the end, when there are two thousand years of heritage behind you, you can't just say "Live free or die" and go your own way. By humbling yourself with memories of the past, you can realize *how* you got here, but more importantly *why* you got here, and what you are supposed to do for yourself now that you *are* here.'

'OK,' I replied, 'tell me this then. Your sisters are over there, shrouded in white, a product of your cultural history. Could you talk them into taking off their shrouds? Is there a "technological improvement" you could offer them to achieve the same end, whatever it is? Or is that too much of an alteration of history?'

'Listen, man. I'm with you. I'm living in the same age as you are, and for whatever religious revival reason, they're living in the past. You know what, though? I'm happy they keep those things on. It's just one more layer between me and them, one more barrier to filter out their incessant bossy commands to me. Let 'em hide behind it if that's what they want. There'll be plenty of good Persian girls at this wedding with burkhas smaller than a handkerchief.'

'If thousands of years of history, both Eastern and Western, hadn't brought us to this point, maybe I wouldn't have met you and your sisters today. Maybe nothing'd be how it is now, and I kind of like how things are. I even like your sisters' burkhas, if I'm being honest. It's kind of what got me talking to them in the first place.'

Darius shook the last of the diminutive green-leaf cigarettes out of a gold-foil envelope. With so many hours left on the trip, he needed to get used to someone else's brand or else he'd be jonesing pretty bad within an hour or two. There was a scheduled thirty minute stop in Rugby, North Dakota, but the train station magazine stand didn't stock specialty Asian import cigarettes.

'You know what?' he said to me, pausing before he lit that final cigarette. 'I think *you* should try and talk them out of wearing their burkhas. You can even use my story. Just don't say I didn't warn you once you finally see their faces. I think there's a reason they insist on wearing them when they don't have to.'

We both crumpled with laughter. 'I'll have to see for myself. We've got hours and hours until Chicago. I'll go back for round two after these cigarettes. Tell me some more Persian philosophy I can use on them.' We laughed again.

'There aren't any good chicks on this train,' Darius said and dragged thoughtfully.

'You're tellin' me.'

The Privilege

Monica Strina

THE FIVE OF THEM had the privilege of being there when their father – and husband – left the torture chamber his body had become. Like a shell it remained, broken, on the white bed.

The elder daughter was standing on his right-hand side, holding his freezing hand. Across the bed from her, the second son smoothed the waves in his father's forehead with his thumb, fighting to stay awake through a night that seemed to have swallowed all.

The others were trying to sleep their exhaustion away.

The younger daughter opened her eyes and saw white tiles and the wooden feet of the bed. She propped herself on her elbow, forcing her eyelids to win their battle against the yellow light.

'What is it?' she mumbled, and already knew. Her mother, too, had awoken.

Around the bed the air hung immobile.

'His apnoeas were lasting longer and longer,' the elder daughter said. 'He went on one of them and didn't take another breath. We checked. There's no heartbeat.'

Sarah, the youngest, stepped closer. She couldn't cry any more: tears weren't even gathering. That wasn't her father. Her father was an athlete and a painter, a man who never lay still.

She took it upon herself to wake up the first son, though she didn't want to. He had only just gone to sleep.

'Sam?'

She put a hand on his cheek. His brown eyes opened.

'Wake up. You have to come.'

✦

People say that, a few seconds before you die, you see your whole life again. That's what made Sarah wonder why it was she who was seeing her father's life right now – his, and hers, and the times the two of them had been as one.

✦

Sarah used to get angry at her father when he drove her all the way to college and then dropped her in the middle of a busy road so he wouldn't have to do a U-turn. She was scared of the cars speeding an inch away from her. Once she panicked and slammed the car door on her thigh and got a bruise that looked like the image of a chrysanthemum on a negative.

Her father had started driving her there after she'd got a bad bout of flu with a high fever and blisters filled with pus in her throat. She kept her eyes glued on her books the whole thirty minutes of the drive and he never said that it was rude of her. He parked on a patch of dry, cracked earth beside the black metal gates of the university, and walked up to the Roman amphitheatre to pass the time until his daughter came out of class and they could go home for lunch.

✦

When Sarah was eleven, her father did something that made her friends envy her for the rest of the time they played together in the garden of their block of flats.

Volleyball was a lot of fun, especially if you had a light ball and an imaginary net; but Sarah and the other children hit the parked cars every time they got a sideways shot, which was often.

'Hey, can I play too?' Sarah's father asked. She hadn't realised he was there.

'Yes!' they all screamed, and the ball started flying higher and they ran faster to hit it.

✦

Sarah wouldn't go near the crabs because they had pointy legs and pincers, but she had no intention of missing a walk in the dark, the first of her ten years. The waves sang a lullaby to the pebbles, rocking them on the shore, and the moon's white tongue shimmered on the water licking their feet.

'Catch him, catch him!'

Sarah's two friends and her cousins were there too, walking and running with their shorts tucked in their pants, but only her father and the most reckless of her cousins dared touch the angry orange spiders.

The seawater was harsh on the bites that the rocks had taken out of Sarah's feet: it made her think about her mother and granny rubbing salt onto the wounds of wriggling eels before cooking them. But she knew that tomorrow the cuts would be smaller, white fading lines.

✦

It wasn't often that Sarah got sick, but, when she did, her temperature climbed until her head radiated heat and her hands and feet froze. She lay in a duvet cocoon all day waiting for her sister to read her a story, for her mother to walk in with a camomile tea and a thermometer.

She was seven, maybe eight, and had caught the measles the time her father came back from the shops with a little pot of glue.

'Here, you can make a collage when you feel better.'

Other times there would be a bag filled with surprises – plastic jewels, balloons, mini playing cards. A key ring shaped like a goblin's head with eyes that moved. A comic book with Sarah's favourite character, so thick it would take her days to get through it.

✦

The table was rickety and scratched and there were patches of paint all over its sides, but Sarah's father liked to draw on it. He let Sarah sit beside him, on the extended bit – a plank of wood that hung from one side of the table and could be lifted to create extra surface – and taught her to always colour in the same direction.

'See? It's nicer this way. Now you can't see any lines.'

He picked up a brush. He had dozens of them, some tiny, some bristly and speckled with grey like an old man's moustache. From his canvas, the pained eyes of St. Agatha pleaded for mercy. Sarah thought it was strange that her father should paint the saint's hair green, but in a way that made her even more beautiful.

✦

Sarah couldn't remember how old she was when her father took her to see the frogs. Six, perhaps?

The pond was an enchanted mirror with a delicate balance. Create but one ripple, and you'll ruin it.

'Look, you can hold them. Be careful not to squash them, though.'

Sarah's smile – a few teeth were missing here and there, and you could already see her mouth was going to be a mess when she grew up – wavered and then widened. The frogs weren't bigger than her thumbnails. Green living things breathing on her hands.

'Wow! Can we take one home?'

'No, we can't. It would die,' her father said, watching his own hand as three frogs leapt across his palm. 'See all this cement?'

Sarah looked. It was grey and hard and it didn't go with the water lilies. She nodded.

'If they keep building here, the little frogs will die. They'll destroy everything.'

✦

Every summer, Sarah's father hitched the camper van to his green Fiat 131 and the whole family got to spend two months at the beach.

Sarah learnt about places where the sand is so fine you can't hold it in your hand for longer than two seconds, and later, in the shower, you find glittering black and cream particles tattooed onto your skin, as if they've chosen you out of hundreds of other bathers.

There were natural shallow bathtubs in the sea, embraced by arms of mossy rock, and, if you stood there, semi-transparent shrimps and fish would gnaw at your feet, making you jump and giggle. You could catch the shrimps by cupping your hands between two rocks, and then use them as bait.

Sand ridges tickled the soles of your feet as you walked on the golden strands of a net cast into the water by the sun. When you were tired, you could lie on a hammock suspended between two pine trees, dangle a leg out and dream about becoming famous.

Sarah loved washing her feet in the sea before going to bed. She loved it because her father would lift her in his arms and take her back to the camper van so she wouldn't get her feet dirty again. It reminded her of all those times in winter when they drove out of town to see her father's relatives, and upon their return she pretended to be asleep so that he would carry her upstairs.

And she knew that tomorrow would be sunny just like yesterday and today, and all she'd have to do was to lower her fishing line near a rock, crouching to see if, amongst curls of dead seaweed, an incautious goby was about to fall for that skewered shrimp.

One time when she had caught nothing all day, her father swam unseen to her fishing line and attached to the hook a mullet he had caught.

✦

When you won a competition or a game at skating, you got a golden star in your helmet. If you came second, the star would be silver; bronze if you finished third.

Sarah's skates and helmet were the biggest things about her. If you didn't look attentively enough, all you could see in between were brown spaghetti legs and white socks. She was proud to say that the wheels in her skates, eight red-rubber spheres looking like bubblegum, had belonged to her father.

'But why are they all worn on the edges?' a friend of hers asked one evening during training.

'Because my dad used to skate down this really steep ramp near his house every day and when he braked he wore them off.'

'Is it true that one time he held on to the bumper of a car, and a wheel came off his skates when the car was going really fast and he ended up like minced meat?'

'Yep! You should have seen the state of him!'

✦

Sarah was afraid of deep water when she was five. She thought it might grab her legs and pull her down, fill her lungs with its translucent emeralds until she was nothing but a wave's white foam.

'Jump! Come on!' her father used to say. He kept afloat by magic, barely moving tanned legs and arms.

And Sarah jumped because he was there. Her inflatable armbands hit the water, splashing blinding splinters into her eyes. She swam like a dog, wrists bent, hands cupped, until she got to where her father was, out of breath and happy.

✦

It had happened so long ago that Sarah could not remember it. But her mother told her. She said that when she – Sarah – was a baby, she had problems going to sleep at night and would cry and cry with her miniature fists squeezed until someone picked her up. You had to be patient, very much so, and that's why she often ended up in her father's arms.

He would circle the kitchen table with slow, steady steps, rocking her. He would walk around it two, five, ten, fifteen, thirty times. He would do it for as long as it took, until Sarah's breathing slowed down, her hands relaxed, and she fell asleep.

✦

In the silent room Sarah looked at her mother's swollen eyes, at her siblings wandering about, straightening things that didn't need straightening, gazing outside the glass sliding door.

She wondered if they, too, had seen what she had, only with each of them as a secondary character. If, like her, they'd just shrunk into children and then babies in their father's arms. And her mother would have seen herself the way Sarah had admired her in that black-and-white picture taken at the beach, with her ebony mane curling in the wind, her smooth bronzed face stunning as an actress's from the nineteen fifties.

Turning towards the bed once again, Sarah searched for her father amongst the crumpled sheets, but her eyes could not find him. And then she gasped. She was looking at the healthy man who used to lift her with one hand and carry her home.

To my extraordinarily creative dad
Thank you

Roosters

Naoimh O'Connor

THEY LIVED AT THE RAILWAY STATION down by the creek, if you could call it living. Mostly, they smoked pot and dressed in high heels and gypsy scarves. They were the oddest-looking trannies we had ever seen. Not that there are normal-looking transvestites, I guess. But sometimes you have an idea in your head about how things should be and when the reality doesn't match, it gets you thinking.

Me and Bob had been hanging around for the summer when we got the brainwave to start collecting the bottle tops for shooting. Outside the station was full of them: VB, Carlton Crown, Fosters, Miller, Bud – all sorts of foreign labels. Bob had made us a couple of catapults by paring down the hoop pine branches we found around the river. He got to thinking that we might practise our shot on the pigeons and when we'd perfected it we could start getting the weirdos. It was that hot now, we couldn't even be bothered going swimming and there was nothing else worth the energy.

We spent two mornings plucking little pieces of metal out of the grassy patch beside the exit door. If we waited until later, it would be busy and we'd attract the lunch-time commuter attention. The guy with the overalls who picked up the trash saw us. But he just smiled and said he was awful glad we were using our time so clever. Bob made stupid faces behind his back. Bob could be an idiot sometimes.

'Bet you can't get him right on the tail.' He had hit the same bird three times and it was struggling now.

We were dangling our legs from the loft-like space between the ceiling and the rafters over the main exit door. It was one of the better hiding spots we had come by when we played seek-out with the gang. That was before they started spending summers at camp. Bob's dad said camp was for wusses and my folks didn't know much about it. Besides, to pass out of school Bob had to sign with the locum every Thursday. Otherwise they'd send him back to the institution.

We were high enough up that no one on the ground paid much mind, unless they were properly out looking. At least a twenty-foot drop, Bob had calculated when he rigged the rope we used to get up and down. But we had to watch our step on the inside because the floorboards were old and loose. Sometimes we fed the pigeons a dose of Mum's intestine mix so we could make them shit through the gaps right down onto someone standing underneath. We took bets on how it would go but it was usually better just to let Bob win.

The heat was vicious and it pushed its way right through the corrugated iron roof into the loft. And practice was slow without my glasses, but Bob said I looked like a nerd when I wore them, so it was easier just to listen to him boast for a bit.

'I can't see him, Bob. How am I supposed to hit him?' I felt the rough edge of the bottle top against my index finger and raised it to one eye like I was aiming a pistol.

'Hey, don't waste it if you're too four-eyes to use it!' Bob reached forward and plucked the weapon out of my fingers.

'I'll four-eyes you.' I grabbed the offending hand and twisted his forearm so it was behind his back. He laughed and wriggled free, his shirt damp with fresh sweat. I jumped on his back and we wrestled for a bit. Just so he knew I only needed the glasses for things that were far away.

We lay flat on our bellies for a while, peering out over the edge, not saying anything. I might have dozed off because the next thing

I knew, Bob was pulling at my t-shirt. But he still wasn't speaking, so I was confused. He dragged me by my sleeve, so we were concealed inside again.

'You ready to try for real?' he said. 'They're sitting targets down there, smoking that shit, they won't know what hit 'em!'

I looked at his pockets, bulging with bottle tops. I reckoned that even without my glasses, trannies were nothing like pigeons.

'Come on.' He didn't wait for me to answer. 'Numbskulls. Won't know what hit them…hit them…geddit?'

He laughed at his own joke.

I said I'd wait until he'd made a few tries.

He started off pretty lame. Tossed one of the tops out of his pocket and let it fall, like he was throwing a coin into a fountain. They didn't even see it land. There were four or five of them down below on the grassy bit, with their pointed shoes and clinking carnival jewellery. They were all wearing wigs and lipstick, except for the smallest one, whose head was wrapped right around in pink fabric. They were smoking, and they slugged from bottles in brown paper bags. It went on like that for quarter of an hour or so, until Bob got bored. He yawned loudly and told me now it was properly time to do something.

'Oh come on Bob,' I hissed 'Let's get out of here. Let's find something else.'

'Look at them, just look.' He wasn't listening. 'They disgust me.'

He wrinkled his nose like he did when he smelled the cat's tail that he had set fire to one time. I didn't say anything.

'Dad says they're not people at all, not men or women.' He talked like he was off somewhere else in his head; it can be hard to get any sense out of him when that happens. 'Says they should all be locked up and have their things chopped off so they don't make no more like them.'

Bob's dad also thought that the aborigines at the supermart were bad as the blacks who should have stayed up in the trees, but not all-out as useless as the chinks who took jobs from the hardworking Australian. Bob's dad didn't work and, far as I knew, he's never met a black man. I wondered how Bob's dad could think so many things that didn't seem to fit. It was better just to listen, though, because sometimes Bob can go a long spell without saying anything much about anything.

'Hey, tranny.'

He was turned around, sitting over the doorway again, swinging his legs. He shot the bottle tops with his catapult one by one, softly at first. But as he called and they didn't respond, he tightened the rubber-band so the caps must have started to hurt on impact. One of the taller ones stood quickly; she shifted her ass like a cow, making me wonder if she was strong like a man or like a woman.

'What you want, little boy?'

Bob blasted one of the tops right at her nose. That made her angry.

'Do you piss with your thing or not?' Bob laughed and reached back to nudge me with his fist. It was a mean laugh, however they pissed. He motioned for me to come sit beside him again. She said something to the others and they turned to stare in our direction.

'Hey, hey, listen to this.' Bob clasped my elbow tight and made another hard laugh before he said, 'Tranny walks into a bar and says, "ouch, that woulda hurt but it doesn't any more", haw haw haw.'

I shook against his arm as he chortled but I was getting the shakes a bit. My guts were in knots, like that time Bob made me do the river rapids with him on his beat-up rower and he knew I couldn't swim. I didn't drown but I had the shits for days after.

The taller one laughed back. 'Funny, got any more or is that it for today?' It was a real laugh, not sarcastic or angry, just bored.

'You think that's funny? What about this?' Bob was standing now and beginning to fumble with his jeans – Bob never wore shorts, even in the middle of July. He was undoing his flies. I pulled away, raising my eyebrows and frowning at the same time. You never really know what's going on in Bob's head.

He dragged himself to standing and started to piss down onto the grass, spraying the sitting group in the process. That stirred them. They stood up like a herd, all in one go, but they didn't scream like girls. They pulled their shoulders back. Like men.

'Bob,' I said to a trouser-leg. 'Bob, I think you should lay off now. You've made your point. Bob—'

'Stop being such a wuss.' He spat at me, his face twisted and angry, and zipped up his trousers. I could tell he had wanted me to piss with him. That way, it wouldn't just be him. I still wasn't expecting it though, so when I opened my eyes again, it took a couple of seconds to realize he had hit me clean across the face with a chunk of wood that had been minding its own business beside him all along. I touched my jaw. There was blood and water and I couldn't feel much else. I presumed that couldn't be good. At first I thought the clatter had unlocked all the sounds in my head at once but it dawned on me that there was something else happening down on the ground. I had to swivel my body slowly to see. Bob was panting heavily, struggling as he tugged at the floorboards around him. He was actually peeling away the top layer of planks.

'Watch your step Bob,' I said but I wasn't sure he heard.

He was hurling the planks at the trannies. They had come too close now to avoid being hit. 'What's wrong with the little prick anyway?' I heard one of them say.

'Yeah, "little" being the word,' another made a little laugh.

Bob got madder then and shouted a whole bunch of things I was too numbed out to remember but I do recall thinking it was pretty dramatic.

A small cluster of folks had been waiting for the midday train and now gathered with the circus of trannies on the grass. They were getting the tracks ready inside, so it was as if the noises were coming out of everywhere then. They all stared up at his contorted mouth and red cheeks as he heaved and exploded a tirade of abuse at their 'fanny faces' and 'twisted excuses of lives'. And then, as we were all stared on, he shuffled another floorboard loose and dredged something from underneath. Bob had showed me the secret compartment where he kept a collection of nudey pictures in a crumpled plastic supermart bag. But now, he was struggling with a thin, rectangular box until it came out from between the floor rafters. I couldn't tell rightly what he was taking out of it until I heard the click.

'A gun?' The words came out slower than they were made in my brain. I was pretty sure I'd be missing some teeth when I checked. I squeezed an eye shut and felt a sticky mess trickling down my cheek.

'Bob, that's a gun!' was all I could manage.

Bob was still railing like a crazy man, his mouth foaming as he fiddled with the catch. He looked like he knew what he was doing too. The commuters gasped and scattered all at once. Someone had called security but nothing moved fast in the heat. The circus group didn't budge though. In fact, they seemed to band together, and all at the one time, they folded their arms across their technicoloured chests. The tall one stepped forward. She was standing just outside at the doorway, looking right up at Bob.

'Hey, hey there, you got no enemies here, mate.'

And just like that, Bob stopped his noise. The tall one raised a flat palm in the air, like a baby being told to wave good-bye to an auntie, or a volleyball player ready for the return. The palm stayed in the air for the longest time, and Bob didn't move. I was busy with my face and the blood and thought maybe he had died or something because it was too quiet. Maybe he'd shot himself silently, but after a couple of seconds he was talking again.

'You shouldn't be here,' he said, surveying them, long and hard. I grimaced and pulled myself over to the edge as well. But I knew not to speak. He seemed to have things to say. 'The world is filthy because of the likes of you.' A kind of vicious rasp coursed through his words. His lips expelled a barrage of expletives, some of which I'd need to research up on to understand.

Then he propped the gun on his arm like he had spent his life practicing. There was a pinging sound, real sharp. In that second, Bob lost his footing and I thought he might fall over but instead he scuttled backwards a few steps.

'Watch your step, Bob,' I was saying but there was still a mess of blood and teeth stopping the words from sounding like anything at all. Without warning, he lost his footing. The gun fired once more, tumbled from his grip and bounced through the loft. I couldn't see where it went because Bob was falling backwards and then he crashed through one of our pigeon-shitter spots close by.

When you're sitting over a railway station exit, watching a group of trannies trying to talk down a boy who's just done his best to kill them and then he falls through the roof, the last thing you expect is for the trannies to rush to help him. But that's what they did. The tall one lunged forward inside the building and slammed against the frame of the exit door. Then the rest of them came after and between them they somehow broke Bob's fall. I squinted through my good eye from where I was sitting, dumb. I was gripping the edge of the loft so my knuckles were white and stiff. Slowly, I noticed that one of the trannies was bleeding and she had whipped the pink scarf from her head to tie it tight around her arm wound.

I could see the tops of their heads real clear. The tall one pulled Bob up close and held his shoulders firm with two big, strong hands. I didn't quite catch the words, but I remember thinking that Bob looked small right then, and that my jaw was beginning to hurt like hell. Things stayed that way for a long couple of minutes. All the sounds had stopped again and I pushed the flat of my hand against my ear a couple of times like I had to when we went swimming and Bob dunked my head in the water. Bob looked up at me through one of the gaps between us, and blinked once, real slow. Then, he looked at the tall one, and blinked the same, hard, slow blink. He shrugged himself free, spat on the ground and walked away in the direction of the creek.

When he was shuffling off along the grassy-patch, I noticed he had shit himself and was limping on his left ankle. The circus group found the gun and someone shoved it into one of the bigger brown paper bags. The tall one looked up at me then for a long time, but I was busy holding my jaw and wondering how long Bob's dad would put him in the cellar for when he found out his gun was missing.

The Road to Valerie

Philip St John

A FEW MINUTES AFTER THE FILM BEGAN a couple entered the cinema. Frank thought he recognised their silhouettes. Carol must have thought the same. She nudged him: the couple was sitting down a few rows ahead. When they leaned into a kiss Carol grabbed her jacket and hurried out the door.

Frank followed into the disorientating brightness of the summer evening. The cobbled streets were packed with young people and loud with music from bars and restaurants. Carol kept walking. Every once in a while she flashed him a glare.

'It's not my fault, Carol.'

'Oh, it's mine?'

'Look, where are we going? How about a drink?'

Abruptly she stopped. They were standing in the cool shadow thrown by a box-like art gallery. Proud head up, slim, tall, she looked well in her hipster jeans and cord jacket. Ever since their youngest had left school, she had put a lot of her increased free time into maintaining her looks.

'Stupid,' she muttered. 'The stupid, stupid idiot.'

Frank hadn't wanted to invite Cian to the barbecue. 'Carol, you've never met the guy. How can you be so sure about this?'

She strode down the wide supermarket aisle, Frank pushing the laden trolley after her. The array of condiments, sauces, dips and powders packed onto the shelves was almost scary. His taste in food had not changed much since he was a kid. Eating out with business contacts, he felt embarrassed that he did not understand many of the words on the menu, and invariably picked an option that contained the words 'chicken' or 'steak'.

It was cool in the supermarket and Carol had dressed for that, in a woollen garment that reached her ankles. Her red hair was tied up at the back, revealing her long, graceful neck. She took down a tin of kidney beans and peered through red-rimmed reading glasses at the contents list. 'I do have a success rate at this, you know. It would be nice if you could have a little faith in me.'

'Success rate?' A memory came to him: a dinner party back in spring. Carol had put a neighbour, a separated man, next to a woman she had met at yoga. 'You mean Dave and…?'

'Mellissa, yes. They're off on holiday together at the moment. She's talking of moving in with him. But you don't find that impressive?'

In her pale green eyes was a gleam of hurt. Frank was surprised that her pairing of Dave with Mellissa had meant so much. Even after thirty years, Carol's formidable air often blinded him to her uncertainties. For most of those thirty years, she had been at home with the kids. There had been a few tries at night classes, and another at a foundation course in art. All those had ended in angry protests about poor teaching or the tedium of the subjects.

'Yeah.' Frank nodded. 'Yeah, Dave and Mellissa was impressive all right.'

He feared she might notice the doubting note he couldn't quite muffle. But her oval face shone with pleasure. 'Oh, it's just something I seem to have. A gift. I don't mean just for matching couples. I mean, for seeing into people generally.'

'Yeah,' Frank said.

An elderly couple pushed their trolley up the aisle. The man was thin and leaned on a cane. The woman was talking loudly, slowly. A stab of fear went to Frank's heart. Until recently, he had never been able to imagine himself as an old person, but now he was as close to seventy-five as he was to twenty-five.

He pushed the trolley to the end of the aisle and down to the shelves of wholefoods at the rear of the shop. More and more of their shopping seemed to consist of organic products. It was difficult to watch in silence as the tastefully designed, expensive packets and cans piled up in the trolley. They could afford it, Frank knew. But he came from a large family, with a father who had never got beyond a low grade of the civil service. Frank's instinct was to be cautious with whatever they had.

Carol looked at the small print on a packet. She had begun to buy the wholefoods when a sinus problem had not responded to conventional medicine. Once a month she visited a healer. Once a week she went to the acupuncturist. Every day she read books about healing forces that eluded the understanding of science. Frank had heard her on the phone recommending the books to friends. Although she had never explicitly said so, he suspected that a few of her friends – the ill, the separated, the lonely – might have begun to turn to her for more than reading advice. One afternoon, he had been out in the garden reading the paper and had gone to the back window to look at the clock on the dining room mantelpiece. Carol was sitting at the end of the table with her friend, Jackie. Both had their eyes closed. Carol's palm was pressed against Jackie's brow.

He had said nothing about what he'd seen. It had saddened and bewildered him. Two old friends, both slim and attractive, dressed in tasteful tracksuits, sitting at the end of a glass-topped table, in a large room that Carol had furnished in a style of comfortable efficiency – two ostensibly wised-up modern women putting their trust in some kind of wish.

It was for Jackie's sake that Carol wanted Cian at the barbecue. Cian! Frank could not see Jackie even talking to him for more than a couple of minutes. Yes, both were over forty and alone, and people that he liked, but that was about all they had in common.

'Wine,' Carol said, and he wheeled the trolley towards the off-licence section. 'What would you like?'

'Beer.'

'I know you like beer. Just now we're looking for wine.'

'Mirabeau.'

She took a step in the direction of the French shelves, then turned towards him and rolled her eyes.

'I wonder if they still make that poison,' Frank said.

As teenagers, Carol and he would share the big, fat-bottomed bottle before going to a party. In Frank's memory, the night was always cold and wet, and the first mouthfuls were horribly sour and sickening. Then you warmed up, almost enjoyed the rest.

He hadn't seen the brand around in years. Even the destitute wanted something classier now. He left the trolley and browsed the shelves with Carol. It wasn't a surprise that Mirabeau had come to mind, really. Ever since they'd entered the supermarket, he'd been thinking of the land on which it had been built – the partly wooded grounds of the Dominican convent school that Carol had attended. Half a dozen times, on cold winter's nights, the two of them had climbed over a crumbled part of its walls and found themselves a quiet place. Back then, there had been no prospect of Carol bringing him to her parents' house to spend the night, as Carol and he had allowed their two eldest daughters to do with their boyfriends. Back then, you had to find a free room at a party, or a dark garden, or the grounds of the convent.

Carol had always professed ignorance as to where exactly the central event of their lives had happened, but by Frank's reckoning the grounds had been the place. Who could tell – perhaps they were now standing over the very spot where she had conceived.

After the shopping came the slow drive through heavy traffic. By the time they reached home and unpacked, Frank had only a few minutes to shower and change. He hurried out to the garden and had hardly got the barbecue lit when there was a ring at the door. 'Can somebody answer that?' he shouted in through the kitchen. Carol was upstairs, readying herself, Judy in the living room. 'Hello, can somebody get that, please?' he shouted again, over the mad barking of Toby. The bell rang once more, and again. Either Judy had her headphones on or she was in one of her moods. Or both. Frank hurried through the house and opened the door.

'Ah, Cian, hi.'

'Howaya.' He thrust a bottle at Frank. 'Probably crap.'

'Oh, I'm sure it's—'

'Early, am I? Bus was actually on time.' He snorted laughter, head bowed, restless eyes avoiding Frank's. In the five years Frank had employed him, Cian had never seemed to meet his gaze. 'Driver was a maniac. Probably needed a piss.'

'Oh. Hello,' a voice said from above them. Carol descended the stairs: a long, slim-line skirt, bare shoulders, a tight, strapped top.

'Oh hiya, hiya,' Cian said, when she reached out to shake his hand. Blushing, he again ducked his head. A thick greying mass of hair fell over his ears and neck and onto the frames of nerdy-cool glasses. As usual, he clutched a bunch of vinyl albums. Cian even brought them to the office. At night, he acted as unpaid DJ in pubs and on local radio.

'You've brought us some music?' Carol smiled.

'No, ah, going on to a party, town, maybe…'

'You're expecting a dull affair here?'

It was the only sign that Carol recognised her mistake. "Come on through," she said. Smiling again, she took the albums from him and admired the covers as Cian followed her down the hall, babbling about Krautrock and Washington go-go rhythms.

The evening was beautiful and warm. Light pouring through the trees at the end of the garden glowed on the faces of guests. Frank stood by the grill, waves of heat and smoke rippling across his view of the people crowding the lawn. He had to admire Carol's ease in company: the hug and kiss, the appropriate questions, the provision of a drink, the graceful departure to see to another guest. Without her social confidence, their life would have been very different, Frank knew. In their early years together, living with two small children in a flimsy house in Shankill, he had often been woken during the night by their noisy neighbours, and for hours would lie awake, fretting that his new business was bound to fail. What would happen then? 'Oh, it won't fail," Carol said, when he revealed the night-fears. 'I trust you, Frank.' And she suggested he bring prospective clients home for a meal, a brilliant move, since many of his customers then were foreign, and staying in hotel rooms, and clearly enjoyed the attentions of a warm, pretty woman. From those evenings came the contracts that helped Frank's company survive.

Through the blurred, smoky air over the grill he noticed somebody wave. A tall, slender woman with a bob of glossy black hair approached.

'Ah, Jackie. Coming to help me burn everyone's dinner?'

Her laugh shattered her air of gleaming sophistication. It was an abrupt laugh, deafening, a release of frustration more than an expression of delight. She always cackled like that, though tonight Frank would concede she had cause for frustration. 'Fuck's sake…' She nodded towards the far corner, where Cian sat alone on a boulder, grinning and tickling Toby's belly. 'You have him in your office every day?'

'Programming genius.'

'I just had twenty-five minutes on the work of Philip K. Dick.'

'That's the abridged version.'

Jackie reached into a paper bag and pulled out a wholemeal burger bun. 'What do you want me to do?'

'Well…' Sweat poured down his forehead. At least some of their guests were experts on food. He needed help, but did he need Jackie? Her voice had the one volume setting: loud. Her eyes were already clouding over with anxiety. And though she was in good shape, a daily jogger, there was about her whole person a terrible frailty of loneliness. It was such a shame: a beautiful, intelligent, kind woman who had never been able to find anyone. Her nerviness, her swings between strident aggressiveness and helpless tears, had driven lovers away.

'No. You should enjoy yourself,' he said. 'But tell you what. Can you keep watch for a minute? I have to pop inside.'

The front of the house did not get the sun in the evenings. When he stepped into the dimness of the living room, he saw that a small fire was burning in the grate. 'Hi!' a voice said, and a plump white hand lifted off the couch. Judy sprawled there, squinting at a music magazine propped on her stomach.

Frank sat in the armchair opposite and signalled for her to take off the headphones. She did and smiled. 'How's it going out there?'

'Overwhelming.'

'Oh Dad, I was on my feet in the shop all afternoon.'

'I'll pay. Better than they do.'

'Everybody pays better than they do. What about Ms. Mystic? Can't she just cast some healthy-option spell?'

Frank scratched at a sauce stain on the thigh of his chinos. His listening to Judy lampooning her mother seemed treacherous, and somehow dangerous. Whenever he objected to Judy's ridicule, though, she laughed and accused him of hypocrisy. And it was true that, more than once, after a few drinks, when he was sitting up watching the Friday movie and Judy came home from the pub, he might have allowed himself to make a quip about Carol's refusal to drink more than a sip of white wine, and her increasingly early departures for bed.

Frank's dad would never have spoken of his wife in such a way. Frank wasn't sure that his dad had loved mam very much: he was at most polite with her, considerate. Still, his parents' marriage had lasted almost half a century. Frank believed that was down to both parties obeying the rules. Stand together, hold the line.

'Your mother is busy, Judy.'

Suddenly he longed for a drink. Jesus, he hated giving parties. It wasn't as if he'd be able to unwind once the cooking was done. He would have to talk to people. That would be all right if they were friends, but most of the guests were either neighbours or people Carol had encountered at yoga and nutrition classes.

So he could not blame Judy for hiding inside the house in her black top and black trousers and pale make-up, listening to music, and eating chocolates she would have got discounted at work in the local shop.

The thought of that place caused a weight of worry to settle over his mind. When Judy had dropped out of college, he had hoped that she would take just a year off. Both her sisters had experienced blips on the way through university and were now in interesting jobs and living with men. But in the year and a half that had passed since Judy had chucked Arts, she seemed to have developed an alarming regard for a group of young people who shared a house near the store, all of them scruffy and unhealthy-looking, and stuck in dead end jobs. While Frank guessed that much of her lauding of her new friends was designed to provoke Carol, Judy's claim that her pals were 'real' and 'total unfakes' unsettled him. At school, she had been a diligent, well-behaved student. For some reason she had since retreated into a rebellious stage she had missed during her years of conformity.

He got to his feet. It wasn't the time to worry about Judy's staying out so many nights a week, or her possibly drug-related mood swings, or the series of mad crushes which had all ended in her being dumped, or the possibility that in one of those relationships she might get drunk and stupid and end up doing what he and Carol had done at her age.

'Dad?' With a pleasing nimbleness for such a big girl, she sat up. 'What is it?'

'Hmm?'

'You've got The Look.'

She had talked about The Look a lot recently. His absent moods, melancholy. Frank always denied anything was the matter. That was his way with disturbing emotions. He fought them off like enemies.

'Oh, all right. Fifteen an hour. Cash.' Judy grinned. 'And keep Jackie away.'

From the shadow of the art gallery they walked down a side street to the quays, and along the river towards the station. Neither had suggested going home. Carol had headed this way. He had followed.

'Forty-three years old. A complete and utter... .' She stopped and put her hands to her face.

'Now, listen,' Frank said. Passersby looked at them. They may have admired his comforting tone: ah, what a gentle, caring man. Yet the moment felt artificial to Frank. Acted. Maybe he was in shock. 'He's a nice fellah, Carol. Weird, I admit. Not great company. But he has a good heart.'

She took her hands from her face. 'Frank, your middle-aged employee is going out with our nineteen-year-old daughter! In fact, he's having a secret relationship with her. Sneaking around.'

'I know, I know.' And Frank was thinking of the dark side too. Cian lived alone in the house his parents had left him. Apparently, it was a dump. Records all over the place, fast food containers. 'But what are we to do? She likes him. And Cian gets besotted by women. You can be sure he's cracked about Judy. I'm not saying that's a good thing, but at least he'll respect her, not like those... .'

All that could be said in Cian's favour, really, was that he wasn't some twenty-year-old cokehead.

'It won't last.' She said it definitively. They had stopped at a pedestrian crossing. 'It's two fingers to us, that's all. We're not "real" enough. But she'll get enough of reality. Another month at most.'

Frank wasn't so sure. Judy's friends would find Cian weird. He would have trouble mixing with them, but not as much as most guys his age. He wasn't really a grown-up, more a decaying teenager.

A train crossed the bridge ahead. They ran in through the quiet ticket-check area, up the steps to the platform and into the nearest carriage. Soon they had left the city behind, the train rushing past a wall over which they could see an expanse of brown sand, a distant line of water, the bulk of Howth Head. Carol said no more about Cian and Judy. She wore her stubborn look. What she had predicted would happen, and that was that.

Her determination brought back those difficult early days in the house in Shankill. He remembered how Carol had done secretarial work at home while looking after the kids. For six months or so she had earned as much as his ailing business. Yeah, there was no doubt he owed her. And looking at the attractive, in many ways admirable, woman sitting opposite, Frank felt a cooling in his blood.

Ever since Judy had left school, Carol and he had been increasingly alone together. They would find themselves still more alone if their daughter continued seeing Cian. Frank could see that future life as clearly as he could the bay: nights in with the TV, meals out, interesting foreign holidays.

Day after day, growing old, alone with Carol.

The train slowed towards their stop. The two of them got up, and a strange feeling passed through him as she walked, a proud, graceful woman, towards the door. A feeling of sadness mixed with fear and resentment. Six months later, after he had first slept with Valerie in her place in Donnybrook, that was the moment he would suddenly recall. The moment when he just could no longer ignore the whispering in his heart. Somehow, without his knowing, the bond he had formed with Carol one night on the cold earth of the Dominican Convent had, like the grounds itself, passed into memory.

Love, Love Me Do

Carmen Cullen

SHE WOULD RING ERIC UP HERE AND NOW, this very minute, and tell him she loved him. Phoebe Dempsey felt a surge of elation almost impossible to quell. He was married, of course, and that was the problem. He'd probably answer her in that annoyed tone of voice of his, but before he'd get another word in she'd put the phone down. She'd have got out what she wanted to say; *I love you Eric,* as quick as a bubble of air shoots to the surface.

It was the most intoxicating thing in the world to be able to declare and the most profound. Her love was inexhaustible and as full of power as a fountain. It was an endless stream of feeling, so much that there was enough for the two of them.

Phoebe tilted her face in the bedroom mirror of her modern bungalow in a remote village in County Kerry. Carefully dyed blonde hair touched her shoulders, and a pretty woman with large, expressive eyes stared back. She might be a housewife stuck in the middle of nowhere and married to selfish Louis, but she wasn't a has-been. Unscrewing a tube of mascara that had come with the week's glossy magazine, she lowered her eyelids. She could leave Louis at this very moment, as a matter of fact, he suited himself so much. She wasn't the person she appeared to be. She was a woman in love.

A blob of thick liquid separated itself from the make-up brush and fell into her eye, making it sting. It watered and reacted so badly, she had to pin her hands by her sides to stop herself from pressing a hanky to it or dousing it with water. She blinked rapidly until the uncomfortable sensation died away.

The rousing tones of the Hebrew Slaves Chorus pepped up Phoebe as she rushed about the kitchen making Mattie's lunch. It was an afternoon snack, really, because he'd sprung it on her that morning that he was staying back to study in the boys' school in the nearest town, and wouldn't be at the gates to be picked up at the usual time.

Between taking the bread from the bread bin and buttering a slice for a sandwich, Eric's face came into her mind.

'Go away, darling, I'm busy,' she whispered, pausing with the knife in her hand, but the face retreated for a moment before floating back. 'You big awkward fool.' Her eyes twinkled. It was true Eric was not that handsome in real life. His chin was too weak for one thing; his eyes could be said to be small and he had a disconcerting habit of messing nervously with his nose, grasping it between two fingers and pushing it about.

But the face that swam before her was as perfect as a film star's. The bugger wouldn't go away and, worse, the imprint of his fingers on her skin and the feel of his lips came back in full force, as if he was there with her or she'd swallowed his image whole and he was bobbing round inside her like a smiling genie.

A Viennese waltz struck up on the radio and Phoebe's heart throbbed. She should be with Eric this minute, in his arms. Instead grumpy Louis was calling her from the room in the house he used as an office. She packed the sandwiches into her bag hurriedly. 'Don't forget to close the door behind you, Phoebe. This place is worse than a barn.'

Her face grew stormy. *Be quiet in there, Scrooge. We can't all be going round cold just because you're too mean to pay for heating.* She had no reason to get so cross because there was Eric once more, winking and laughing. 'Let him groan. We have our own bit of private fun together and he can't spoil that.' It was enough to be able to imagine his voice as he nibbled her ear.

'See you later, Louis. I'm off to collect Mattie,' she cried and, to please the cross fellow, she held the key of the door in an open position with her fingers so that it would click home smoothly.

As she stood beside the car, heat from a burst of sunshine caused Phoebe to open her coat. Turning round to peel it off, she caught sight of her husband's face in his office window and waved at him. The angle of the sun showed him clearly; that perfect dimpled chin of his and full lips she had to pretend were Eric's when they searched for hers. She couldn't make out the words, but a scowl had transformed his face and his eyes flashed with anger.

He knew something. She lifted a hand to smooth back her hair. It was a gesture to calm herself, to act as if everything was normal, and she mouthed back, 'I can't hear what you're saying,' shaking her fashionable hairdo. It was just as well her attention was otherwise engaged because the man who had her heart in thrall had driven into the yard. Mind you, there was nothing unusual about that. Louis and himself had always got on, and recently he seemed to be never out of the place. Hopefully, her husband hadn't observed her wide smile and the telling seconds she delayed, drinking the darling in before driving off. A black cat leapt across the short avenue as she swung out, making her brake sharply. Good luck, or maybe it was bad. She checked the mirror briefly, rubbing her lips together to bring out their pink lipstick glow.

Thoughts of Eric came and went, as she headed away from the village towards the boys' school. Bramble-covered stone walls and thickly packed hedges rolled by. She hummed a song. The telephone poles along the grassy verges seemed in tune with her bright mood, listing this way and that like soldiers at ease. Sometimes a neighbour passed and raised a hand in greeting, and once a young boy herding sheep across the road in a fast-moving stream caused her to halt. A sudden disturbance had made a sheep buck and break away, darting pale-flecked eyes in her direction and butting the car. Phoebe jumped out to direct it back into the pack. She was surprised a short time later when she saw the front of Eric's old jalopy in her rear-view mirror.

'Well done, you boyo. You were quick off the mark this time,' she smirked and flicked her hair forward. Her painted nails dipped out of the car window provocatively and cold travelled up her arm. Eric eased his car around hers before parking in front.

'We can't keep meeting like this.' She had tilted her chin, glancing in amusement at the gangly man who slipped into the car beside her. He barely sat on the edge of the seat.

'You could be right. God knows what trouble you'll get me into.' His eyes shifted. He rubbed his hands together and grimaced.

'Excuse me for speaking. Are you not going to say hello?' She smiled back primly. It was the least he could do. Her becoming hair was flung back when she reached down to turn the key.

'I'm sorry, Phoebe, I shouldn't have said that. How about a kiss to make up?' She saw his eyelids flicker and felt a warm touch as his fingers released hers. He leaned across and gave her a quick peck on the cheek. The movement towards her had caused the seat to click back, and he pressed a foot into the floor anxiously.

'You're an awful woman, do you know that? And you have me worse.' Softness came into his eyes. 'It's great to see you all the same.' A loose button on his jacket, hanging by only a few threads, had swung out when he reached to caress her knee.

'Things are looking up so. Your wife is falling down on the sewing, I see.' She cocked an eyebrow, fingering the swaying button.

'Who says I can't sew for myself?'

His endearing mouth lifted at one side in a grin and he tickled her waist. Her annoyance evaporated when he leaned forward to kiss her on the lips. She melted. It was a poor way to describe the effect Eric's kiss had on her, she often told herself – too commonplace, because, really, there were no words to explain the sensation of old-fashioned swooning, as if the real her had disappeared. He couldn't be experiencing anything like this kind of passion with his wife. She didn't even have a decent pair of tits, for God's sake. She might be able to ride a horse like a bird from those posh stables of hers, but what good was that to you in bed? She had Eric where she wanted him all right.

A fly buzzed in the open window and landed on the dashboard, but she hardly saw it. Eric had started to make her legs weak, nuzzling into her neck. The only thing that stopped her fainting away with passion was Mattie's sandwich box falling off the dashboard onto her lap. The door at her side nearly opened when Eric pushed her against it, and in the distance they heard the sound of a car approaching. 'Don't stop. To hell with it.'

Her plea was impossible and he sprang upright, hitting the sandwich box with his elbow. 'This is ridiculous. We can't keep it up.' Exasperation crept into his voice. 'I knew I should have driven on,' he added gloomily. 'For your sake, for my family's sake, we have to try and stop. Mary will find out.' The last words were tagged on as an afterthought, but Phoebe knew he had hesitated at using his wife's name. She watched him rub his face to remove any trace of lipstick.

Coward. The thought leaped at her unexpectedly. 'Whatever you say,' she murmured. She had to soothe him because that neighbour's car was clanking past and the driver glanced right in at them and nodded. 'Louis has a meeting in the hotel tonight and I can slip out.' She grinned, turning towards him graciously. 'We'll go for a spin and talk about it then.' Making sure the nuisance neighbour was well gone, she grabbed Eric's hand to press it before he eased himself out of the car. 'Wear that after-shave lotion I like.' She leaned towards him, aware as she did so that the top button of her blouse was open suggestively.

The following evening Phoebe was surprised to hear Louis conducting quite a lengthy conversation with Eric on the phone. They were speaking earnestly, and more annoyingly, her own name was mentioned a few times. True, Louis and Eric were good friends. She could feel herself beginning to boil inside. She was being treated like somebody of no importance. Something needed to be done about this situation, all right, and she was the one who would do it.

'Are you there, Phibsie? I'm getting some supper before going to bed,' Mattie called from the kitchen at the same time.

'Why don't you try the cheesecake I left in the fridge?' She made her voice chirpy. It was funny. She had to as soon as her son called her that pet name. A nervous tick started in her cheek as she joined him. Poor boy, caught up in the middle of all this.

As she drove to meet Eric, in contrast to the journey she'd made earlier that day, Mattie's face hung in the air. It wasn't just the boy saying goodnight at his bedroom door, but a series of pictures. The lad was running towards her with a cheeky grin on his face, or grabbing her and swinging her around without a care in the world. Something was wrong with her coat, she thought, as she took a bend sharply. She glanced down thinking it must be caught in the door and yanked it firmly. There was a grinding noise in the engine she hadn't heard before. Maybe these were signs she should turn back. When she pulled in to release her coat, a thin mist drifted in, wetting the side of her face like tears.

The first returning to her senses after she and Eric had made love in the car was the penetrating pain of a gear handle in her back and cramp in her left side. The closeness of the night, that mist and the quiet spot they had chosen to park, under a canopy of dripping trees, made her feel submerged, like some creature given sea-lungs, drifting along in a make-believe world. She breathed lightly, marvelling at the simplicity and yet the strength of her feeling; that she had so much to give and that, however much she did, it would be renewed for the next outpouring. She stretched her hands over her head.

'I love you, Eric.' Her very heart was singing.

'You're too good to me. I don't deserve such a beautiful woman.' Eric's light voice rasped like a crow's when he tried to speak softly. It was one of the things about him she didn't like. Squinting up to look at his adorable slim nose, she was surprised too that from this angle it looked as sharp as a knife.

'I'm missing you too much. I want more than just this,' she declared. It was just as well to get it out. The air had to be cleared.

'Did you ever think nothing good lasts forever?'

'Don't be ridiculous, Eric. I wish you wouldn't talk like that.'

It was important to keep her voice even. Some kind of pressure was making him ratty. It wouldn't be the first time he'd been so negative. A sudden fall of residual rain in the trees hit the car like pebbles. 'Let's forget I said anything, OK? ' Her small hand crept into his big one.

Eric was staring ahead. In the half-dark, his eyes had a glassy look as if she could see right through them. *He's brooding too much*, she thought. Why had she opened her big mouth? She'd gone too far, all right. He had spoken like this at other times, but then his eyes had softened and they'd fallen into one another's arms. He hit the steering wheel abruptly. From the dripping trees, the sound of a bird disturbed in sleep reached in.

'There's no future for us. It was obvious from the beginning this was going to have to stop,' he choked. There was a clicking sound at the back of his throat.

'Nobody has it as good as we do, Eric. It can't get any better than this,' Phoebe said, grasping his wrist tightly. Her power of speech seemed to have gone. This was definitely getting out of hand. She reached her fingers up to stroke his cheek. 'We love each other, don't forget.' Her voice had a whining sound. The headlights of a car, passing along the lane by their spot, probed the darkness and swept the trees in front. Her hand fell on that loose button, worrying it. Rough tweed grated against her half-naked shoulder.

'I don't mean to hurt you, Phoebe, but it really does look as if we must call a halt. Something has happened. I didn't want things to end this way. Honestly.' His voice was silken, smoother than she'd ever heard it. If only she could stop the clock right now before the next words.

'I'm not listening.'

'My wife is pregnant. I thought I'd better tell you before it showed.' He took her hand.

Phoebe gasped as if air was punched out of her. Her mouth hung open because she really was under water and those gills she'd imagined before had clammed up.

'How could she be?' she croaked. 'You're not supposed to be

sleeping with her.' A trickle of rain started down the windscreen glass and trunks of trees showed, as if the whole outside was pushing in.

'Bastard,' she whispered. It was all she could think of to say. 'I hate you,' she added helplessly, to give strength to her words, grasping on to them as if they were a sword to swing through the dark air.

Trees

Rachelle Dolan

'VIRGINIA, what took you so long?'

I had just emerged, wild-eyed and frazzled from the front door of my house.

'I'm going to kill that stupid, stone-age steamroller…'

Lila looked at me sceptically. 'Are you complaining about your printer again?'

'That printer has the detail of like two pixels per inch!' I cried, my voice breaking in desperation. 'It's like it's printing Braille! It ruined my paper. See?' I said, waving the pages in her face. She took them from me to look. 'Don't laugh. Do you see all the dots that are supposed to be words?'

'Why is the ink purple? And why does your computer paper look like parchment?'

'How should I know? I think my mom must have bought paper bulk a decade ago, and we're still using it.'

'It looks really old.'

'Well, the printer's the real problem!' I said. 'It wrecks things. I looked to see how my paper was coming out, and it was emerging in a light purple colour. This is what I'm turning in, Lila – a piece of yellow paper with purple dots on it.'

'Okay, look, get in the car,' Lila said. And – actually being kind for once – she helped me carry and load my things into her trunk.

'We're late,' she added, slamming the trunk shut. 'By the way, Ron and Jake are in the back seat.'

'Why?'

'Because they're helping me with my tree presentation.'

I got in the car warily and looked behind me. There were two green triangles in the back of Lila's Honda.

'Um, guys?' I asked, deciding to get straight to the point. 'Why are you dressed as green triangles?'

'We're trees.'

'Yeah, trees.'

'Ah, trees,' I said.

'Yes, trees,' Lila said, getting into the car.

I twisted around in my seat to get a good look at them. They were both rolled up in huge swathes of green felt, and looked like two bolts of disgusting-colored fabric. The cardboard cone hats on their heads (which looked suspiciously like birthday hats spray-painted green) didn't help matters.

I cocked an eyebrow at them.

'You guys are dressed up as trees because Lila made you, aren't you?'

'Well, yeah,' Jake said, grudgingly. 'How did you know?'

'It's as revenge for writing "loser" on her face two nights ago when she fell asleep at your house. I'm right, aren't I?'

He nodded gloomily. Glancing over at Lila's profile, I saw that the thick, dark letters spelling "loser" on her forehead were still visible against her skin. Two days before, she had gone to Jake's house to work on math homework with him, had fallen asleep, and had woken up to find marker all over her face. It was one of Jake's extremely hilarious practical jokes.

'Wow, that pen was really strong, wasn't it?' I said to Lila, trying not to smile.

Lila merely shrugged indifferently, her eyes on the road.

'Yeah,' another voice drawled from the back, 'that ink isn't going anywhere.'

This was spoken by the smaller, lighter green tree, which started chuckling merrily. This lighter tree was Ron. He continued laughing until Jake pulled at the end of his fabric, causing it to cut off his air supply. There were choking sounds from the backseat.

Lila looked at me then and said, in a voice more annoyed than was necessary, 'That's not why they're dressed as trees.'

'Then what's it for?'

'Remember?' she said, tersely, casting me a look. I smiled back in what I hoped was a sympathetic manner. I think that it must have come out like a rabid dog laying eyes on a bone though, because Lila turned away from me quickly, looking alarmed.

'My presentation, about tree planting in the woods,' she said. 'You know the trees, right off campus? It's today. The landscape architect is going to be there and everything.'

Ah. Now I was getting the picture. Lila, who is on every kind of committee imaginable, had somehow got herself made president of the Palisades High Woodland Society. I remembered her telling me how she was going to give a presentation to the Parent Teacher Association on how they should plant more trees in the little wooded area off campus. This was certainly a subject that needed to be discussed since the patch of woods next to Palisades currently resembled a small-scale landfill, but I didn't really see how Ron and Jake dressed as trees was going to help.

I decided to ask Lila, delicately, why she was using them. I put the question to her, trying to rein in the rabid dog look.

'It's not just them,' she said, suddenly angry. Apparently, one comment like this was all it took for her to snap. 'There are five more of them. They're going to move around demonstrating the different lay-outs of trees, while I talk about them with my PowerPoint.'

I stared at her for a moment, in shock. The idea was terrible, even for a Lila under stress. Had she become completely unhinged? Was the stress of the school year finally getting to her? Had the ink Jake used to write on her face actually seeped into her brain?

'I see,' I said, trying to sound supportive. 'You're going to have seven people, dressed as – trees – dancing around while you give your presentation. No, that's nice. Really. I think that's such a *creative* way of doing things…'

'Well, the landscape architect apparently likes "creative" things,' Lila snapped. She seemed aware that the tree idea was ridiculous, but was fighting to remain calm. 'And you know, Mrs. Dunson is going to be there too, all the way from her district office. I think she might *like* the idea.'

Mrs. Dunson, Lila's special friend, was an administrator for the school district. Lila had gotten to know her through all her committee work, and I knew that she was expecting Mrs. Dunson to write her an effusive letter of recommendation for her college applications. Lila was nervous about this because Mrs. Dunson, while writing outstanding letters, and only to a select number of students too, sometimes snuck in details about the student which weren't the most flattering. Lila once told me Mrs. Dunson had written a letter for a guy in debate club telling all about how he had once crashed his car into the wall of the school. He had offered to organize a community mural where he had crashed to cover the damage. Not a bad story, but not something you necessarily want broadcast to the admissions officers at Harvard.

Yes, I could definitely understand why Lila would be nervous if Mrs. Dunson was going to be at this meeting. When we parked at the school, I gave her a smile and wished her luck.

'Oh, it'll be fine,' she said, distractedly. Jake and Ron were starting to rehearse their tree movements in the wide spaces of the parking lot.

'Okay, well, see you at lunch. Oh, wait a minute – where's my paper?' I said. I had been rummaging around in my backpack and the trunk of Lila's car, looking for it, but couldn't find it. 'Where is it? I thought it was here.'

'Your paper?' Lila repeated. She shrugged. 'I thought you took it with you into the front seat.'

'No,' I said. I felt myself starting to panic. I rifled through the trunk again, checked the back seat, the front seat. I got down on my knees and looked under all the seats in her car. There was nothing there but empty soda bottles and granola bar wrappers.

'Oh, crap,' I said. '*Crap.* I must have dropped it on the way to the car.'

'Oh no!' Lila said. She looked at me sympathetically. 'Hey, I know,' she said brightly. 'You emailed it to me this morning, didn't you? You sent it to me at five a.m., so I could read it, remember? I'll print it out for you during first period, while I'm running errands for Mr. Grenville in the office, and that way you'll have it by third period.'

'Oh, *thank* you.'

'Easy Virginia, no need to scare people.'

'Sorry,' I said, trying to calm down.

'Don't you worry, Virginia, I'll get your paper. Now wish me luck – my presentation's second period! Where are you second period, by the way?' I thought this question was a little odd, because she should have known that by now.

'I have a free study period. I'll be in the library.'

'Oh, yeah – well then, you'll probably see my presentation,' she said, again, very brightly. 'That's where we're having the meeting.'

First period passed peacefully, and by the time second period rolled around, my heart had stopped beating from the shock of losing my paper. I was just on my way to the library when I felt my cell phone vibrate against my leg. I stopped walking, and pulled it out. Someone had sent me a text message.

'Sorry to spring this on you,' it read, 'but I have been trying to print your paper out and the office printer is being difficult. Do you think you could cover my tree presentation for me? Jake's bringing the computer with the PowerPoint, and the slide projector's already set up, so it should be easy. I would do it myself, but I want to get your paper printed for you. The pres. is only five minutes long. It shouldn't be a problem! Thx! Lila.'

I stared at my phone, wondering if I was seeing things. What did she think she was doing? The printer was giving her problems? I thought about what this meant. Well, it was a plausible excuse. Last year, the students at Palisades had rung up a huge printer cartridge bill and so the administration had outlawed all printers except the one in the office, which was guarded by a particularly spiteful, vindictive secretary. I had tried to use it once, and I still get nightmares about the way she spat in my face and practically clawed my eyes out just for asking. It took guts to use that printer. It definitely took guts. If Lila was in there, doing her best to print my paper, it would not be that hard for me to do this one little thing for her.

At this point in my thoughts, I noticed a pervasive green glow horning in on my field of vision. Looking up, I realized I was now in the midst of a forest. The trees were gathering their heads towards me and leaning in like I was the centre of a football huddle.

'Hey!' I yelled to the triangles. 'Don't – *surround* people like that. It's disturbing.'

All seven green triangles laughed happily at this, and then Jake cried, 'Take her into the library! She's the presenter!' and all of a sudden the green felt rolls were pushing me down the hall and through the library's double doors. Luckily, at the barcode detector thingy they couldn't all fit, and I walked in ahead of them, while they banged into it as a group and started milling around like creatures in a video game.

Jake followed me through and steered me towards the conference area at the back. There was a projector set up there, and a laptop.

'See?' he said, gesturing. 'Lila must have been in here earlier. It's all set up to go.'

I looked warily at the laptop. The first slide was up on the screen. It said, 'Designing Palisade Parkland: Three Options for Landscape Improvement.'

I stared at it, horrified. I had to dump this terrible title on an unsuspecting group of school officials? And a landscape architect? (Even if she was "creative", she would probably still want to vomit from the slide – not to mention the seven trees.) I noticed Lila hadn't put her name on the slide, a sure sign she wasn't proud of her work. The slide had a picture of a fir tree on it – a completely uncalled-for picture of a fir tree in an alpine meadow somewhere. There was no conceivable way fir trees in alpine meadows had anything to do with our school.

Jake was still at my elbow. When he saw me hit the "next" button to look at the rest of the slides, he pointed to the screen and said, 'Now, see this, Virginia? Lila already told me. For each of these three slides she's showing, we trees will move into a different formation.' I read what was written on the slide and cringed.

'What is this,' I asked, 'some kind of code?'

'No, Virginia,' Jake said, shaking his head forgivingly at my mistake. He looked at what was written on the screen and nodded sagely. 'That is a kind of conceptual name for the design Lila was going to talk about. It's perfectly clear if you know designer lingo…'

'But how am I supposed to know what it means?' I cried. 'It's meaningless! What am I supposed to say to the' – and I lowered my voice, because they were filing into the library – '*important* people coming in here?'

'Use our formations as a guide,' Jake said, gesturing to his fellow felts. 'We know what we're supposed to do for each design concept, so maybe you could just describe to the audience what we're doing.'

I swiftly turned my back on my growing audience and yanked Jake by his fabric so that he turned with me. 'So, you're telling me,' I began, through gritted teeth, 'that in order to impress these people, I should flip through these inane slides while attempting to explain what six of your track buddies, dressed up as trees, are doing parading around the library?'

'Oh gosh!' Jake exclaimed, looking at his watch. 'The meeting's about to start, and you're up first. I'm going to go sit by the other trees.'

I watched him scamper off, a lost, desperate expression probably registering on my face. I turned back around to my audience, attempting to put on a welcoming smile. I saw the president of the PTA, Marcia Kripp, coming towards me.

'Virginia, is that you?' she said, sounding mildly surprised. 'That's funny. We thought it was going to be Lila giving the presentation.'

I saw, beyond Marcia, Mrs. Dunson making her way into the library. She came over to our little group and took a front row seat for the presentation.

I shook my head in answer to Marcia's question. 'No, something came up. I've, uh –' I realized then that I had to sound plausible in order to pull this thing off. 'I, well – I have been working extensively on this project with Lila. It's, um – very exciting what you've been planning for the woods.'

'Well, then,' Marcia said brightly. 'I'd like you to meet Tiara, since you are so interested in our project. She's our volunteer landscape architect. She's taking time out of her busy schedule to do some *pro bono* work here at Palisades.'

I turned to greet Tiara. She gave me a kind of awestruck, magical smile and then, with the arm she wasn't using to toy with her scarf (she had been toying with it ever since she walked up to me, like it was continuously moving out of place), she said, 'Virginia. How lovely to meet you. I should tell you, I love the spatial flow of this room. And the windows over there, opening out like that into the forest beyond – well, I'm surprised that the architect of this building was so interested in integrating indoor and outdoor space. How lucky you are to be a student here. It really is something of a *masterpiece* of modern architecture.'

I looked at her, nonplussed. The first thing that had tipped me off that she was a nutcase was the wide-eyed look she was giving me. Now, while going into raptures about spatial flow and indoor and outdoor space, she was trying to tell me that Palisades was a "masterpiece of modern architecture"? Every student at Palisades – not just me – will tell you that this is complete, absolute crap. Tiara obviously hadn't been here like the rest of us when the top floor sprang twenty leaks after the windstorm last year, or when a chunk of concrete fell off one of its corners, revealing a gigantic rat colony in the insulation material of the walls.

As Marcia and Tiara took their seats, I thought that if she was the one I was meant to impress with this presentation, it was going to be a piece of cake. Dancing trees would be right up her alley.

Mrs. Dunson, from her seat in the front, was now glancing at her watch and then up at me, looking expectantly at the first slide. 'Shall we begin?' she said. 'I understand there is a student giving us a little presentation before we start our meeting.'

Well, this was it.

'Hello, everyone,' I said, smiling nice and wide. Then, remembering that people got scared when I did that, I instantly stopped. I glanced over to see what the trees were doing and saw that they were all in a clump about ten feet away from me, respectfully silent.

I groped around for an appropriate opening line, looking down at the laptop in front of me. I said, 'The title of today's presentation is, "Designing Palisade Parkland: Three Options for Landscape Improvement".'

I glanced at my audience, allowing the title to burst on their imaginations in all its glory, and saw six heads looking dully back, waiting for me to continue.

'So, anyway,' I said, getting rid of the pine-tree-in-alpine-meadow photo, and replacing it with the second slide. 'Let's move on to the first suggestion Lila has – I mean, we students have – about the design layout for the woods.'

The first design idea, a few well-chosen words, was all there was on the screen for this next slide. The six heads stared at it. It said, 'Nodal Centers of Interest.'

I turned towards them and announced: 'NODAL CENTERS OF INTEREST.'

I heard a rustling to my left, and realized that the trees were moving into their first formation. They had divided into groups of twos and threes (there were seven of them) – and each group had put their backs together, and then stuck out their arms, in a supposedly graceful manner.

I gave my enthralled audience a few seconds to absorb this stunning visual representation. Tiara in the front row looked like she was about to pee her pants. 'Oh!' she gasped. 'A forest of trees!'

I was glad she had gotten the gist of the felt objects, and now thought it would be safe to continue without my audience getting up in a body and walking out on me.

I switched to the next slide. Again, the words had a great impact on the six heads. Marcia Kripp was squinting really hard at them, as if she were reading ten point font.

Again, I announced the phrase. 'PROGRESSIVE CHAOS.'

I looked over at the trees, wondering what they were going to do with this one. I jumped a little when they all suddenly dropped to the ground like jungle cats, and one by one started to stretch out on the ground, as if they were some kind of aggressive vine. When they all finished stretching, each tree got up, and started whizzing around the room like they were on roller skates. There was another startled, 'Oh!' from Tiara. Everyone watched the seven trees until they came to a stop a minute later.

I sighed, deciding anything else I might say could not top the trees' spectacular performance, and pressed the enter key one more time on the laptop.

'And finally,' I said, trying to remain serious. One more to go and then I would be home free. 'TOPOGRAPHICAL FLOW LINES.'

I turned and crossed my arms, wondering how the trees were going to deal with *that.* I shouldn't have worried. They formed a straight line and each one crouched so that they were at a different height than the next. Their line-up looked like something out of *The Sound of Music.* I decided, by far, that this was my favourite.

After allowing everyone a few moments to let this final tree scene sink in, I moved to the last slide, where the words "The End" and the unfortunate fir tree from the beginning were plastered on the screen.

Tiara, who was still looking at the trees and applauding loudly, was far and away the most impressed with the presentation. Everyone else was giving us only a light smattering.

'Well, that's about all from the Palisades Woodland Society,' I said. I noticed Jake had come forward next to me as if he wanted to say something.

'Oh, and I was instructed to tell everyone,' he said importantly, 'that the society is working on more concrete presentations of these ideas, but since they are only in the conceptual phase at this point, we thought we'd only give you the broad artistic ideas today.'

I nodded along with him, as if I had been at the meeting where they had made this decision. When it became clear that Jake had nothing else to say, I went with him and sat down in the audience.

As the meeting wore on, I thought how lucky it was that Lila had removed her name from the PowerPoint.

Three minutes before third period, I stood anxiously outside the door to my English class, waiting for Lila to come with my paper. She had better have it, I thought, after I gave that presentation for her.

She didn't come until about twenty seconds before the bell rang. She rushed up to me, her dark eyes beaming. She had that smug look on her face, which usually means she has just won a scholarship or gotten an A.

'Hi Virginia!' she gushed, grabbing me by the arm. 'Thank you so much for covering that presentation. I don't know what I would have done without you! Jake said the landscape lady loved it.'

'Oh yeah,' I said, nodding. 'I think Mrs. Dunson thought I was some kind of lazy idiot, though.' Lila winced. 'But better me than you,' I continued. 'You're the one that wants the recommendation from her.'

To my surprise, Lila's face became flushed. 'Yeah,' she said, looking pleased. 'I actually just ran into her. She's going to give it to me on Friday.'

The bell rang. 'So,' I said, quickly. 'Did you fix the printer? Did you fight that secretary and print my paper?'

'Yep,' said Lila, not meeting my eyes. She pulled some stapled pages out of her notebook and thrust them at me. Immediately after, she bolted into the classroom before I could thank her.

I looked down at what she had left in my hand and goggled.

The paper was yellowed, like parchment, and the words were faded, purple dots.

The Topaz Bistro

Niall Duff

Monday

Sean arrived at the bistro just before twelve o'clock. He rooted in his pockets for a crumpled piece of paper, the scent of basil and ginger filling his nostrils.

'Excuse me, I'm looking for The Topaz Bistro,' he said to the Latino-looking waitress, as plump as she was pretty.

'This is it, you're here.'

'Oh. It's just there's no name outside, only–'

'Yeah, we're having the name changed. It's getting painted today.' She handed him the brunch menu.

'Actually, I'm here to meet Ray.'

'Oh right, you're here for the job.'

'Yeah.'

'He'll be back in a few minutes. If you just want to sit over there, I'll bring you something to drink. Tea? Coffee?'

'Can I get a cappuccino please?'

Sean watched the boxes pass by his table. Just how much lettuce can one restaurant consume? It's only a garnish in a place like this, he thought.

The rain beat down outside. A bus moved by at walking speed.

The top deck was a row of see-through patches wiped clear in the condensation.

Sitting there waiting gave him time to think about things. Did he really want to work there, or anywhere? Most other people in college weren't working. But they were living in their parents' houses, whereas he had a bed-sit to pay for, and books to buy. The library was inadequate; anything he wanted was never there. He had chosen classics because it seemed like the least employable degree, but now at the end of second year he was forced, by penury, to work, a situation he found to be somewhere between ignominy and tedium.

Ten minutes later, one of the half-doors swung open, walloping a chair in its path. An aristocratic but ravaged man strode through the bistro, passing right by Sean's table, running his hand through his messy hair as he went. At the waitress's signal he swung around to face Sean, his grubby long coat flapping like a sail.

'You're Sean?'

'Yeah, that's me.'

'I'm Ray. Follow me, please.'

His manner, though brusque, was somehow less rude coming from him than from someone neater. Sean followed him through the bistro into a corridor from which opened a dull grimy room, with only a roof-window. They sat at either side of a Formica-topped desk. A small fan in the wall made a faint whirring sound, though it seemed by the stench of stale carpet that the fan was bringing nothing in or out of the room.

'So it says here you were working at Café Montreux from May to October of last year, and then you've accounted for the last three months. But can you tell me what you were doing between October and March of this year?

Sean felt choked on the inside. He was struggling to remember the right version. He had put together a lot of *Curricula Vitae* over the last few years, all of which were fictitious. His task was hampered by Ray's breath, an odour reminiscent of fermented potatoes.

'Eh, I, I was just working in a shop at the weekend, because of college.'

Ray kept reading the paper CV in his hand for a minute, and then looked up.

'OK Sean, it's like this. What we do here is mostly lunches and dinners. Nobody comes here for breakfast, just coffees all morning OK? And the way we work is Alicia stays serving on the floor all the time, while Jeff operates the dumb waiter from downstairs, where most of the food gets made.'

'The dumb what?'

'The dumb waiter. It's a small elevator for putting the food in.'

'Oh yeah.'

'But what I need right now is someone else to work between downstairs and the main floor of the bistro. Are you up for that?'

'Yeah, sure. I've done it before,' Sean lied again.

'OK, you can start tomorrow then, around ten o'clock.' Ray stood up to leave. 'Just wear something black; we're not too fussy – a bohemian haunt. We get a lot of artists and actors.'

'OK, see you at ten o'clock tomorrow then.'

Tuesday

Sean arrived for his first day of work dressed well enough to be visible to customers, but badly enough to soak up the rancid by-products of the kitchen. It had stopped raining. This time the girl offered him a handshake.

'I'm Alicia.'

'Sean.'

'Have a coffee before you start. Here I'll make you one.'

'Thanks.'

Sean sat down on some boxes in the kitchen, wiping his eyes. He hadn't been up this early since school, five years before.

'So Alicia, where are you from?'

'I was born in Peru, near the capital, Lima, but my family moved to Birmingham when I was twenty.'

'Oh, right. Are you over here long?'

'I'm here a year now. I came here to study at the drama school.'

Sean started washing the same lettuces he had seen pass his table the previous day. His hands felt like cement gloves in the gelid water.

'That must cost you a fortune.'

'It does. But I'm following my dream. That's all I can do. And if this place closes, I will have a big problem to find enough money to pay the rent.'

Sean was carrying catering tubs of sauce down to the main kitchen downstairs, and answering her on every return journey.

'Sure there's no chance of this place closing. He's only just taken me on.'

'He didn't tell you about Friday?'

'No, what happens Friday?'

'A Health and Safety guy is coming here, and Ray is worried that he'll be closed down.'

'Really?'

'Have you seen the state of the cellar kitchen?'

'Yeah, I suppose it's a bit wrecked, though the customers seem to think this is a very cool place to eat.'

By the time lunchtime arrived, Sean was helping Jeff with everything in the kitchen, though they hadn't even spoken to each other yet. When the busy spell wore off, he had been back upstairs a while when he heard the intercom of the dumb waiter making a fuzzy rasping noise, then a voice filtered through.

'Dude, I'm down in the kitchen. Come on down.'

Sean descended with the sense of duty of a man new on the job. When he rounded the bottom of the stairs and went in through the kitchen door, he noticed that the lights were off. Jeff, who could easily be described as 'runt of the litter', was cowering behind the door, mumbling,

'Dude, come in. You gotta see this, dude.'

Sean walked slowly into the darkness of the kitchen. One dim light was left on, that of the microwave oven.

'Watch this, dude.'

Still puzzled, Sean looked at the microwave and noticed that there were two eggs each in an eggcup with faces drawn on them, rotating steadily inside the glass door. *Splut*! *Splat*! They blew up that instant and Jeff reeled around the kitchen laughing. Sean returned upstairs, puzzled.

'Sean, can you bring these to number six?' Alicia said, handing him two plates just as he reached the top of the stairs.

'Sure.'

On his return to the coffee machine, he quizzed Alicia.

'How long is Jeff working here?'

'He's here only a month. He sometimes sleeps downstairs, even overnight.'

'No way.'

'Really. Once I came in and he was sleeping on a mattress he'd made from raw dough. His body left an impression on it like a plaster cast. Ray went mad. Jeff said it was a soft bed. We had to make more fresh bread, though.'

Wednesday

Sean arrived at the bistro with a feeling of cosy familiarity, as though he had worked there for months. He went straight to the coffee machine and fixed himself a double espresso, then turned around to face Alicia, who was juggling some oranges.

'Aren't you afraid Ray will come in and catch you?' said Sean.

She laughed. 'He's never in before midday. And he always walks straight by without looking, talking to himself.'

They swept around the tables, and set knives and forks for the lunchtime customers.

'How long is this place here anyway?'

'About fifteen years, I think.'

'Yeah?'

'But Ray took over only five years ago, when his studio building was demolished.'

'He was an artist?'

'Sculptor.'

Sean went down to the kitchen. Jeff was standing with his back to the door chopping something. Tinny-sounding music leaked from his earphones, and his baseball hat crushed the spring of his ragged curls. He still didn't speak to Sean.

When the lunch orders stopped, the pair of them stood there in the fluorescent glare, one deep-frying prawns, the other splattered in cream cheese. Jeff took off his earphones and turned to Sean.

'Hey dude, check this out.'

He fumbled at the door of the dumb waiter.

'Dude, if you take out the middle tray, you can get in, and go up to the top, scare the shit out of Alicia. I've done it before, loads.'

Sean looked into the dumb waiter. It seemed to be just about big enough to take a person, if you scrunched into a hunker ball.

'Eh, I better not, coz I've just started, and if Ray–'

'Come on, dude. I've done it before. Ray's gone to the Oyster Festival anyway, so he won't be back today.'

Sean hesitated, then he thought of the face of Alicia laughing as he appeared upstairs in the place of a cannelloni order. He lifted one leg in, bent his neck and squeezed the rest of his body across, filling the space like a contortionist in a box. As the doors closed, Jeff grunted,

'OK dude. I'm sending you straight up.'

Sean made a muffled response, while Jeff replaced his earphones. Jeff continued chopping courgettes as before, the tinny music now screeching under his pâté-soiled cap.

Upstairs, Alicia took a coffee to a seat at the window, enjoying that space between lunch and dinner, when the remaining trickle of customers had been served. She wondered if they would pass the health inspection. There seemed to be so many things broken downstairs, and Ray's tradesmen never appeared. If the bistro closed, she might have to leave her drama course. Worse still, she might have to go back to Peru to work again, at preparing Capybara meat. Her reverie was interrupted by the sound of Jeff's footsteps. He walked by the dumb waiter and over to the coffee machine. He glanced up at Alicia, who had turned back to gaze at the street. He looked at the dumb waiter and then at her again and finally shuffled back downstairs with a coffee, five sugars sweet.

Thursday

Round about twelve o' clock, Ray strode in, wide-eyed and animated.

'Alicia, I've some good news. A friend of mine who runs the gallery is giving us some paintings to hang and sell from here. It will impress the inspector no end.'

He took a swig from his hip flask, and just as he waited for the coffee machine to quieten for Alicia to respond, Jeff appeared from the kitchen below.

'Uh Ray, we've no bleach, and uh, there's something up with the dumb waiter. It won't go up and down any more.'

'Ah Jeff, I was just saying to Alicia that–'

'Excuse me, say, do you have a rest room I could use?' blurted a rotund tourist who had just walked in from the street.

'Well, are you a customer here?' said Ray.

'Not today, but I've–'

'I've never seen you before.' By then, Ray was draining his hip flask of the last drop.

'But I–'

'Oh go on then,' said Ray, searching the presses for any dregs of whiskey.

Down in the kitchen, the floor tiles were beginning to moisten, but not from the mop-water. The tile grout was porous and absorbing water from the sewers below. The room smelled like an abandoned abattoir. Jeff had recently stuffed raw meat in the vents of the kitchen in the hope that the stench of rotting meat would flow around the flues of the air-conditioning, thus polluting the airspace of the customers.

Back upstairs things were starting to hot up. Ray was on the phone.

'Yes, yes, of course we'll organise that for you, no problem. It's the week after the Jean Tinguely Exhibition, so we can easily fit you in.'

Alicia was rolling in the awning to overcome the dullness of the evening. When she came inside, Ray turned to her.

'Well, since that waster Sean has not even had the decency to phone in sick today, he can consider his job gone. So if you see him, Alicia, will you–'

'Uh Ray, the um, the bathroom is flooded. What'll I do?' said Jeff, appearing with a plunger in one hand and an aubergine in the other.

'Jeff, I've a meeting at three with a guy from the Arts Festival. Can you close the toilet until I come back?' said Ray, moving briskly towards the door, scarf flailing.

'But we can't just close it, Ray,' said Alicia, 'it's too busy, we'd have to–'

'Just tell them to go across to Brannigan's. He's got more toilets than he has customers,' cried Ray, as he went out the door.

After Ray had left, Alicia scowled, and Jeff slouched away, his prawn-sodden apron trailing after him like a perverted bridal train.

Friday

At eleven o'clock Ray burst through the door, a tornado in tweed. He hadn't had a drink yet.

'OK Alicia. Lynch is coming at three o'clock – that's his name, the inspector guy – and we have a huge lot to do before then. Where's Jeff?'

'He's downstairs.'

Ray walked into the kitchen to find Jeff fumbling with the parts of a blender.

'OK Jeff, Lynch is coming at three, the inspector guy. We don't have time to clean this place properly before then. So I want you to hide everything that's broken in the broom cupboard and then lock it before Lynch gets here.'

'Uh, OK.'

Ray lifted a slime-covered mat and exposed a collection of tiger prawns wrapped in filo pastry which had swollen to double their size in the moist conditions of the cellar. Ray's eyes started twitching.

'JEFF! WHAT THE HELL ARE THESE?'

'Uh, I think that guy Sean–'

'Just bin them. And anything else you see like that, just bin it, or hide it in the broom cupboard.'

'Uh, OK.'

Lunchtime came and went, and for a Friday it was quieter than usual in the bistro. This gave Ray more time to plan his encounter with Lynch. The hour from two until three evaporated, and Alicia found herself shaking hands with Lynch, a genteel man in a dated jacket. He sat with Ray at Alicia's favourite window table, the one that helped her dream. Ray sucked a mint and looked sycophantic, while they went through the procedural paperwork. And then the time came for the detailed inspection of the whole bistro. Ray shadowed Lynch around the place like a grovelling lemming. They got to the kitchen, where Ray winced on the inside as Lynch ticked the boxes on his clipboard. After ten minutes they returned upstairs and sat down again. Alicia looked on, worried. Lynch spoke.

'OK Ray, the good news is that you have passed the inspection, but only barely. There are a few detailed points that I want you to remedy before my return visit in three weeks' time. Part of the problem is that all the cellars in this area experience leakage from the water table. But there is a building specification to cover this with which you must comply.'

Ray winked at Alicia. They were in the clear. Alicia smiled from her eyes, and offered Lynch an Irish Coffee. Ray went to check for a spare bottle of whiskey downstairs. As he walked into the kitchen, his eyes flashed onto the dumb waiter, and he remembered Jeff's complaints about it. He grabbed a potato masher and started prising open the doors, while holding the switch with his other hand. There was a slipping, clicking noise. He searched through the warped and broken utensils until he found what looked ideal: a jemmy bar. This time he held the switch with his left hand, and levered the jemmy bar down hard with all the strength of his right hand. *Crack*! *Twang*! The thin cable inside had unhitched and the doors sprung open. The dumb waiter was full of clothes and runners. Ray was baffled.

He went to take out the clothes, and realised, on a second glance, that it was Sean.

'JEFF! COME HERE! QUICK!'

There was no reply. Ray started tugging Sean out carefully, trying not to bend any limbs the wrong way. Not knowing anything about pulses or first aid, he thought about carrying Sean's limp body up to Alicia. She'd know what to do, he thought, but what about Lynch?

Lynch was by now looking for the toilet. He went downstairs and pushed the first door on the right, thinking it was the toilet door. Instead, he found Jeff sitting in the dark on an upturned bucket, eating chicken wings and surrounded by broken plates and swollen tiger prawns. Clapped-out blenders lay with mangled utensils, and the floor was a beige carpet of cooked rice leftovers. Lynch stormed off to find Ray.

As he reached the top of the stairs, Ray had Sean lying on the coffee counter with his heels dunked into a cheesecake, and was attempting to give him the kiss of life. Alicia looked on, at Ray struggling with Sean, at Lynch returning, stern and puzzled, and at Jeff following, with Cajun sauce smudged around his mouth.

She wished she were in Peru again.

What Was Lost

Ruth Patten

Silvia

Millicent was difficult on the phone. I am sure she just wanted to talk about herself and those irritating – oh so talented – kids she never stops rattling on about. Of course my problems are too real for her to have any interest in discussing. Everything is *Guys and Dolls* this, Sky Masterson that. What else did I expect? Last year I never stopped hearing about *The Pirates of Penzance*. Every year it is the same. She acts as if the school musical production is the centre of her entire existence. I am almost glad Tim has turned their spare bedroom into a study; at least I won't have to hear every tiny detail of rehearsals if I am staying with Lydia.

Terrible business all this sleeping in spare rooms. I would move into a hotel if all the money wasn't tied up right now. I explained that the lawyers are in the process of dividing the assets and I am a little light on currency right at the moment. The rates in Dublin hotels are shocking as well; it is safe to say a lot has changed in Dublin in my thirty year absence. François took care of everything on our infrequent visits before. Now he is taking care of his pneumatic secretary somewhere in the Algarve. Hardly likely they are kipping on friends' floors. But patience, patience; I will get what I deserve in the end. Thirty years cannot so easily be pushed aside.

Lydia seems a nice girl; although I have to wonder what a thirty-five year old woman is doing unmarried, not even living with a man. Or woman – I am quite open minded. I only want to see her escape her mother's dull life. What on earth is she doing, teaching like her mother? Nice apartment though, no doubt Tim helped with the mortgage. And new as well, since she's only home. She did spend all that time in Italy. I wonder if there is a story there. I'll have to ask. She's a good girl to let me stay. I have not seen her in – oh, it must be ten years? She had just come back from her travels and was still sore from her split with that boy – what was his name? Oh I can't remember, Martin or something. He really cut her deep. I remember being impressed at the time that she had gone on without him. He was a cad to abandon her in Thailand like that but she bucked up and went on to Australia. She reminded me of myself back then. I was proud.

And now we are both single – oomph what a horrific word – and will be living together back in Dublin. How utterly depressing. Still, it is only for a short while. When I get my money I am going to find somewhere new, somewhere much more fabulous than this overpriced dump, maybe Berlin or Venice. I shall take a lover and be scandalous. Not that running away with a Frenchman wasn't scandalous in the Ennis of 1968! Oh yes, I will show my true colours, make that man wish he never set sight on that anorexic snippet. You know, I might take Lydia along. She would be useful, considering she has Italian, if I remember correctly. And Venice is far more glamorous than anywhere in Germany. She can escape her mother's life once and for all. She could take a lover too; it would do her the world of good. And if nothing else, Millicent will be speechless for a week!

✦

Goodness knows what is wrong with that child. She has had a face on her that would stop traffic. I could hardly have done anything to upset her, my comments were purely constructive. She cannot honestly be happy living like this. Perhaps she is having difficulty at the school. Why anyone would spend their lives in the company of children is beyond me. One's own I could understand, but other people's? That lawyer was meant to call this week. Where did I put his number?

Lydia is a pleasant enough girl, and was certainly welcoming in my first two weeks. She even cooked dinner every night and we would open a bottle of wine and talk and talk. I did think it sad that she gave up Italy to return home to Dublin. But she insists that teaching in Ireland is much the same as teaching in Italy only with more rain and less bureaucracy. Don't you miss the sun, the life, and the men? I asked. She blushed, if such a thing were possible for a thirty-five year old woman and replied that home has its rewards. Foolish girl. There are no rewards with Irish men who would pass you over for a cooked dinner and the sports insert in the paper.

No, there is nothing like a Mediterranean man for putting fire in your heart and nothing like a wee Irish girl to put fire in their loins. When I said that she had to leave the table she was so embarrassed. Imagine! That is no way for a grown woman to behave. One would think she has not had a man at all. Perhaps it has just been so long she has forgotten. Oh, François was something else; even when I had suspicions he was eyeing up the maid, he had a way to get me on my back in half a heartbeat. For all his faults we had our moments. And I do miss him terribly, or maybe it is the passion I miss. Now that he is off sharing it with some limpet on a beach and I am sharing an apartment with a woman who is wasting her youth.

At least I know that I never wasted mine. I wrung every second out of my formative years: we travelled, partied, saw so many things. And that was back in the seventies before these 'low fare' airlines came along and ruined everywhere slightly interesting by giving the uneducated masses the chance to see them. I heard they have closed off the Parthenon. Shocking. I remember when François and I shared a cigarette sitting on the steps looking out from the Acropolis over Athens. That was an experience. Now people queue to walk past it and take photographs. Life is for living, that was all I was saying to Lydia, and I did mean it kindly. She seems such a sensitive girl. She'll never find a man at this rate. They won't want to look at her for much longer.

I spoke of our move to Venice as soon as I had decided she would do as a companion, and, I must admit, it was after I had consumed a number of glasses of wine. She was not as grateful as I expected but politely feigned interest. I suppose she feels she is humouring me. More like her mother than is necessary, that one. She will find her manners once she sees the apartments I have been looking at. The agent was very keen but I will have to keep him at a distance in case I sign anything in a fit of excitement before the money comes through. The pictures were gorgeous and just perfect for my plans. When Lydia sees them she will drop everything, I know it. No one could possibly choose a life here in dull Dublin over vivacious Venice!

✦

Millicent suggested I should, 'contribute to the house,' as she put it. As if I wasn't feeling unwelcome as it is. Lydia has been practically impossible to live with recently. And I know she has been buying the cheap plonk in Lidl instead of that fabulous wine merchant I told her about. I cannot possibly drink such horrific grape juice and she knows it. She just sits there with her rubber pasta and smirks as she takes a sip. Well, let her. If she wants to contaminate her body with such filth, go ahead. She is definitely showing a masochistic streak I had not anticipated. Of course, such things are to be encouraged in one's private life, but to treat a guest like this is scandalous. And now she has gone running to her mammy.

Of course I was not intending to stay over two months here in Ireland but there have been some technicalities and the lawyer has explained that it is going to take more time. Not that this will be enough for Lydia. She has been leaving the jobs section around the sitting room and making wide circles of ink around those she feels would suit me. Ha! Secretarial, administration, temping. She even had the nerve to imply I should go on the dole. I cannot begin to form a response to that.

What on earth has got into the girl? She is in desperate need of someone to come along fast and knock some of that tension right out of her. Someone who could distract her for a while until the settlement is agreed. I wonder who would be up to the challenge. Certainly not any of those drips calling themselves men in that school of hers. That overseas investment agent might do, but I definitely got the impression that there is a little missus hidden away somewhere, not that the man would be liable to forget that if given the opportunity, but Lydia is inexcusably moral about such things, so better to find someone more suitable.

It is a pity my lawyer is based elsewhere; he would be perfect for her. Goes straight for the kill does that man. Utterly intoxicating and so charming. Not even Lydia could deny him. I certainly couldn't if he came along. Of course, I was always faithful to François – more is the pity. If I had known he would betray me for an adolescent titbit I would have acted quite differently.

✦

Lydia

I don't know why I agreed to have Silvia in my flat. It was a favour to Mum really; she is an old friend of hers after all. They have some history; God knows what, and it means that whenever Silvia comes along everything gets thrown up into the air. I was just getting everything in the flat the way I want it as well. I got some lovely things from Habitat and the most gorgeous cups and blankets from Avoca. They really brighten the place up. Of course, as soon as Silvia saw the living room she said I was living like a spinster. I told her there is no such thing in this day and age and if I remain single for another ten years it won't matter. She had to reply that no man would want to stay the night; she said the décor would remind them of their maiden aunt, all flowers and trinkets.

What would she know anyway? She thinks she is some sort of authority on the subject of men – what a joke! Sure, hasn't her husband just run off with some young one? They are living in tax exile or something over in Portugal. She talks about it like she has no problem with it. That is called denial. But was it really a surprise? François always had the roving eye. Oh yes, they had their passions or whatever she calls it. When they were staying in our spare room at home we could hear their passions at all times of the day and night. But he was never one to see a pretty girl walk past and not chase after her. Sure, there were plenty of times he would come on to me, and I only a teenager. My mum says he tried it on with her every chance he got and I'd believe her.

Silvia is driving me up the wall with all her talk of moving to Venice and starting a new life. I have no idea why she wants me to come. I get the distinct impression she is as fed up with me as I am with her. She just doesn't understand how content I am here with my little life. I have my flat and I have work. Yes, the kids are little demons but I get on well with some of the other young teachers and they have all invited me to their weddings. Who is to say I won't find Mr. Right then?

Silvia talks about seizing the moment and getting out there, but I have been out there. In Italy I lived with two Italian women. I used to hear all their crazy stories and sometimes I would meet them or people from the school in a bar or whatever. They were always such fun nights. I never really felt I could go out with any of the men there, obviously. Mum and Dad have always been very clear on wanting me to marry an Irish man. I have to respect that after everything they have done for me and they were so patient when I ruined my chances with Martin, and his father a judge. Dad had high hopes there. I should have looked the other way; it was only a holiday fling with a local girl, which hardly counts. I hear he is a barrister now.

Silvia is living in a dream. She is starting to grate with all her so-called helpful advice. My life is just fine the way it is. She has to stop taking my Mum and me for granted. She is eating me out of house and home and never puts any money towards the groceries. Her lawyer has not contacted her in weeks about the divorce. That really cannot be a good sign. Of course, the money is not going to come. Dad said there's no way François hasn't hidden it all away somewhere. She employed that lawyer because she fancies him, but he's probably in on it. He flirted a little bit with her and she trusted him completely – so pathetic.

My life is perfect. Sure, I cannot wait to get married and have a few babies. I think maybe two, a boy and a girl. I hear Martin's wife had a daughter a few months ago. That makes three he has now, far too many for me. I may be thirty-five but it's not too late. When the right man comes to find me, I'll be here.

In Between Dreams

Maria Pace

Laurie wakes up early to the sound of her alarm beeping. She feels dreadfully tired. As if some vitamin or mineral is missing from her body. Still drunk with sleep, she entertains the idea of lying in bed all day long. She cannot remember anything important she is supposed to do. But luckily for her, she had good dreams. Without the power of these dreams, the pleasant feelings they have left floating in her head, she would have little incentive for getting up. But there was something. Something about flying in a pink nightie and some sort of escape. And a campfire and somebody's eyes and a sense that she was in charge.

Remembering these things is enough to get her to swing her feet out of bed and put them on the floor. But things go downhill from there. Whenever Laurie flies in her dreams, it is as if she is swimming the breaststroke in the air. She is able to dodge objects and propel herself higher or lower in the sky at will.

But physics aren't the same during waking hours, and on the way to the bathroom, she bumps into her desk chair. On the way back from the bathroom, she crunches her pelvis bone into the corner of her dresser. When she examines her reflection in the mirror, her hair seems brittle, grotesquely static and a bit greasy near her scalp. She finds it impossible to pin back in an attractive arrangement. The skin on her face seems drier and paler than usual. While she is chewing her cereal, she bites her cheek.

The dreams have dissolved and she is thinking of class, which she must hurry for, and of the slip she received yesterday in the mail notifying her of a package she needs to pick up at the post office.

She walks as fast as she can from her flat toward the bus stop and is nearly there when she sees the bus turning out of the lane. She has missed it. But she thinks perhaps she can catch it before it enters the main road. She breaks into a run. The bus pulls away. Pre-menstrual cramps grip her guts. Dangerous ones like dark rich soil for potted plants. Or like an ancient starfish plucked straight from the ocean and rolled over slowly by a mack-truck so that all the saltwater squeezes out of it. Laurie breathes deep. She will be late for class.

While she waits for another bus to come, she sneaks a warm palm through the buttons of her coat and under her sweater and presses it over her abdomen. A mother and son come to the bus stop. Laurie assumes they are natives of the Dublin suburb. The mother is holding a white paper bag. 'Would you like a moo-fin?' the mother asks her son.

A *moo-fin* Laurie repeats inside her head. As the mother and son bite into enormous puffy chocolate chip muffins, Laurie imagines a Holstein cow with huge udders swimming in the ocean with a shark's fin strapped on its back. Her stomach growls. She clenches her jaw.

A young woman in a pretty red coat stands along the curb. Her purse hangs heavy on one shoulder and she holds doggedly on to a plastic shopping bag that looks as if it will break open soon. A car pulls up to the curb and the passenger door is pushed open from the inside.

A young man is driving and the woman gets in, releasing the bags onto the floor of the car. He leans over and kisses her cheek. She slams the door. Music spills out of the car.

Laurie watches the turn-signal blink orange in the cloud of the car's exhaust. As the car vanishes, she imagines the man and the woman going home to make tea and walking around their house in warm socks. She imagines the woman putting the contents of the bag away inside shadowy kitchen cupboards with other cans and bright-labelled jars and spices. She imagines them watching movies lazily in the dark under a large puffy blanket.

The bus comes. The driver frowns and says nothing when Laurie shows him her student pass. She climbs the stairs to the upper deck. Before she is able to sit down, the bus is moving and Laurie feels like a plastic figure in a snow globe that has come unglued and is being shaken by a relentless kid. She imagines the driver smiling as he watches the passengers being tossed around in the Closed Circuit Television footage. She staggers into a seat.

Along the way, the bus stops at a traffic light near a stone cathedral. In the churchyard under a stand of towering trees, Laurie sees an old woman sitting on the grass. She is wearing a pale pink kerchief on her head and the point of its triangle rests on her grey coat along the sloping curve of her back. She has set up a picnic in the style of a young girl's tea party. She has spread a cloth about the size of a bath towel and Laurie can see little things resting on it, maybe a sandwich and a thermos cup and a packet of cookies. Beside the woman sits a tabby cat, white with brown-grey patches. Its back is curved too and Laurie can see that it is fat and sleek. The woman's crooked hand goes over and over the cat's glossy back. Laurie presses her forehead to the glass as the bus moves forward and she wishes she could get closer to the woman; or be the cat under her crooked hand.

Laurie slips into the back row of the dark auditorium. She settles into her seat and lets her eyes adjust to the darkness. She unzips her school bag as quietly as possible and smoothes down a new page in her notebook. Her muscles soften and her heartbeat slows. She enters the world of the professor's presentation: old faces, oil paintings in blood red and deep greens and sketches in coffee-stain brown. She is engrossed in her notebook, in the past. She likes looking at things that have already ended and making sense of them.

After class, Laurie slowly zips her notebook into her bag. She is very calm. She leaves the auditorium behind a girl and guy who are shoving each other and laughing. Laurie walks in the trail of their perfume and cologne.

At the post office, she takes out the slip notifying her that she has received a package from home. She queues behinds a woman in high heels who seems to be in a hurry and to know exactly where she will go once she finishes her business at the post office.

When it is Laurie's turn, she gives her slip to the lady behind the counter. The lady takes it and turns to go back to the shelves where the packages are sorted. She slams the parcel down on the counter and adds Laurie's form to a pile of others. Then she says nothing and waits for Laurie to go, her head tilted as if she wishes she would disappear so she can get on to the next customer. Laurie says thanks quietly and turns to leave.

She takes her package to the park with a tickling feeling in her throat. She walks through the gates of Saint Stephen's Green and finds a place on a bench beside a man wearing a brown wool coat. He is looking down at his folded hands. Laurie puts the big padded envelope on her lap and studies her best friend's handwriting. She is a little afraid of opening it because she does not want to know what is inside. She likes that it is there, unknown, on her lap.

Then she can't wait any longer and tears it open. Inside, there is a copy of her favorite magazine. She stares at the bright shiny cover photograph. There is a couch upholstered in green silk. The lady stretched on the couch is wearing a long yellow dress. Her feet are bare and she is smiling. The wall behind the couch is covered in bold black and white paper. In a vase on the table in front of the couch are lovely long-stemmed roses with yellow-orange petals that look like they could be made of velvet.

Laurie's eyes move to the flaked red nail polish on her own fingers, and annoyance interrupts her pleasure. She begins biting her cuticles.

A card falls from between the pages of the magazine. Its red envelope stands out against the golden white pebbles on the ground. When Laurie bends down to get it, she notices a strand of hair hanging from the envelope. Her friend had sealed the letter with a sticker, and one of her hairs had been caught under it. Laurie pulls it between her fingers. And now, because her friend knows her so well and thought to send her this magazine for no reason other than the fact that she knows she likes it, and because Laurie can now see her hair, which has traveled all the way across the ocean without her friend, Laurie cries.

She does not care about the people walking by or the old man sharing the bench. She opens the envelope and reads her friend's letter. Her tears keep coming down and feel hot on her cheeks at first but leave trails that grow cold.

She thinks of her friend's house, the tangle of it, the smell of coffee grinds and banana peels in the kitchen trashcan and the scent of laundry detergent that always lingers in the bathroom. She thinks of the flowery blue-green water stains on the bathtub and the view out the window from her friend's couch when they sit in the living room on quiet Sundays with their legs folded under them. Laurie wipes her cheeks with her scarf. She tucks the card and the magazine into her bag.

She goes to the library and sits at a study desk. She pulls her books from her school bag, but she cannot bring herself to open them. She watches people for a while, all of them strangers. The serious ones, the ones who seem to send and receive endless text messages, the ones she can see outside through the window walking hand in hand, the ones she can tell through the glass are laughing and shouting in the open.

She cannot concentrate. The room is too warm and the air seems fuzzy and the lighting is too yellow. She opens a book and bends over it, but the words lie flat on their pages and she decides to leave.

She wanders into a few shops, looking for something to inspire her, but everything is too expensive. She is holding a cookbook with bright pictures that remind her of what it feels like to wash dark red cherries in a colander under cool water. Or to open the oven and have heat flood over her skin and wiggle the lose strands of hair around her face.

Laurie holds the book and thinks: Isn't there something else I should save my money for? She thinks of bills and debts.

Worst of all, she imagines buying the cookbook and not using it at all. She imagines it never delivering the alluring promise it had suggested on the shelf before it was hers. She puts down the book.

She boards the bus back home and gets off into the darkness. The day is over. Laurie imagines herself being videotaped each day. She sees herself scurrying in fast-forward back and forth between the same places and not being sure what happens in between. She doesn't know if the idea of walking over the same paths over and over again in life makes her feel encouraged or hopeless.

Inside her bedroom, she slides on her pajama pants. The worn cotton is very soft on her legs. She pulls the pajama shirt over her head.

She moves her toes in the darkness under the covers. She lets her cheek rest heavy on the pillow and opens and closes her eyes, listening to her eyelashes moving against the pillowcase. The wind sings around the corners of the building and she remembers that she is on an island, that the sea is not far away and that she is part of it all, the motion and the flux, and her breathing becomes even and she is free again to look for unknown things in her dreams.

Does Not Compute!

Mark Stewart

THE MEN BUILDING THE NEW HOUSES on our estate forgot to lock the door of the hut they used at break-time. Mammy didn't allow me to play on the building site but Captain Kirk said, 'Boldly go where no boy has gone before'. Inside the hut were piles of cement bags, a gas cylinder with a hob and a kettle, and a few shovels and trowels: nothing interesting enough to get in trouble over. The big stupid robot from *Lost in Space* told me to go home.

'Does not compute!' he said.

I should have listened. But a blue and yellow Leeds United holdall called out to me. 'You want me,' it said. I crossed the carpet of old newspapers, rancid milk cartons and biscuit packets, opened the zip and emptied it out. Leeds was my team.

I couldn't believe what was looking up at me. She was gorgeous. Her red-painted nails were holding open a shiny silver jacket. She had nothing on underneath. A quick flick through the pages nearly made me believe in Santa Claus again. I had never seen anything like it – there were more pictures of my silver lady inside, without her jacket. And she had friends. And they had nothing on at all.

My heart pounded harder than the Six Million Dollar Man's as he was breaking up. For the past while I had been obsessed with setting my eyes on naked female flesh. It was in short supply in those days where I was growing up. Right enough, there was the odd stolen look at the BBC when Mammy and Daddy were out at choir practice and Uncle Brian's *Sunday World* sometimes had pictures of ladies in bikinis, but this was the real McCoy. This was a thing called *Penthouse.*

All of a sudden I got the feeling of a slimy claw stroking my spine. I thought that I was being watched. My heart nearly gave out. I checked around outside but there was nobody watching me – only God.

'This is stealing,' he said. 'And if your Mammy finds it, you'll be killed.'

But the warm glow I got in my belly whenever my willie was hard bubbled away like red-hot lava and made my mind up for me.

'Finders, keepers!' it decided.

I stuffed my new girlfriends under my vest and took off for home faster than Speedy Gonzales.

Getting past Mammy was no problem. She was in the scullery, frying mince for Daddy's dinner and peeling potatoes at the same time.

'Take your wellingtons off and don't be dragging muck into my good clean house,' she said, without looking around.

'I have them off,' I said, using them to conceal the lump in my duffel coat. 'Can I borrow the record player? I want to read.'

'Don't have it up blaring,' she said. 'I'm sitting down to watch the news when I've your father's dinner cooked. It'll be the first time I'll have sat down all day.'

I dumped my wellies under the range, ran upstairs and locked the door. My bedroom was like an ice box. When the record player was warming up, I plugged in the convection heater. I didn't want to have to go under the covers and I wanted to be naked, to feel as bold and wild and free as the time me and the boys had gone swimming naked in the summer when there was no one on the beach.

I pulled over the curtains, put on the reading lamp and put *Live and Dangerous* on the turntable. The music kicked in. Thin Lizzy filled my bedroom with ballsy attitude. I stripped naked and lay down on the eiderdown with silver lady half-dressed beside me and went at the *Penthouse* like it was a Christmas selection box. First I flicked through it to see where the best stuff was. Then I took my time with each of the girls, keeping the best for last – I liked having something to look forward to. By the final track on side one, when Phil Lynott was asking the audience to clap their hands to *Rosalie*, I was getting acquainted with my own personal Rosalie, who filled the centre pages with her wonder. We were lost to the world, my Rosalie and me, the two of us flying headfirst through space to that moment of pure joy in the heart of the sun.

Then there came a knock at the door and that slimy claw was back, raking my spine. It dragged me out of Rosalie's Technicolor embrace and sent me crash-landing head-on back into my dreary grey reality.

'Are you at something not right in there?' Mammy said.

Not right? I thought, confused. Then I almost died with the fright. I thought: 'Fuck! She knows. How could she know? Oh dear God, strike me down dead, I'm destroyed.'

'I thought the bed was going to come down through the ceiling,' she said. 'What in God's name are you at?'

She tried the door handle. For a horrible second I thought I'd forgotten to lock it. I thought my world was going to end. I could see her head coming around the door with that same look on her face of anger mixed with disgust and disappointment that she gave me when I was caught nicking a Mars bar out of Scally's shop, only a hundred times worse.

'Open this door! Don't have me raising my voice to a locked door.'

The guilt that I always felt when it was my fault that she raised her voice took hold of me. It had got to the stage in the past few months where I could do nothing right in her eyes. Everything I did annoyed her. But I was fighting back. And now, like a rat trapped in a tight corner, I went for the jugular.

'You wouldn't be talking to a door only for you're so stupid,' I said, turning up the volume to hide the noise of me scrambling into my clothes.

'Don't you be so cheeky,' she said. 'How dare you talk to me like that? What kind of an ignorant thick lump am I rearing?'

'I didn't ask you to have me. Or rear me, neither.'

'What did I ever do on you to make you so spiteful?'

I could hear in her voice that the tears weren't far off. I put the volume down slightly.

'OK? Will that do you?'

'Let me in!' she said. 'What are you at?'

'I'm head-banging,' I said. 'Like you know I always do to Thin Lizzy.'

I hid the *Penthouse* under the pillow. She gave the door handle a few good yanks to show me who was boss in the house.

'The headboard is nearly through the wall,' she said.

There was a tone in her voice that I hadn't heard before. She was nervous of me, embarrassed maybe. I knew then that I had her beat. I opened the door just wide enough to talk to her.

'This is an adult-free zone,' I said. 'I'm old enough now to have my own private space.'

She looked me straight in the eye.

'And you're old enough to know the difference between right and wrong,' she said. 'Shame on you, you dirty wee scut ye. Shame on you!'

'Does not compute! Does not compute!'

The robot was back in my head. I was confused. I didn't even have a name for what I was doing. All I knew was that it felt really good. How could she know whether what I was doing was right or wrong? She didn't have a willie, so who did she think she was to be putting shame on me?

I was scared that she would tell Daddy. Daddy and me got on. He brought me to the pictures and he would take me up the mountain with him now and again. Right enough, he sent me to bed when there was serious kissing and ladies taking their clothes off on *Rich Man, Poor Man* but we didn't fight. He wasn't as perfect as Pa Ingalls on *Little House on the Prairie*. But one time when Murder Mulgrew threw a stone at me and split my head, Daddy gave him such a clip on the ear that he never came near me again.

The following Sunday, when we were doing the dishes after dinner, he said to me: 'Brendan, we'll take the dog for a walk.'

'You're grand, Daddy,' I said. 'Sit and read your paper. I'll take him.'

'We'll go together. We need to have the talk.'

The talk? I wondered. The way he said it was like he was telling me he had just run over my bicycle.

We took our regular route around the shore. The tide was out. The mudflats and the sky were having a competition to see which one could be the greyest. He made small-talk with me about school and football. He was nervous. He ran out of things to say to me and went off into his own world. Then he took the ground out from under me.

'Brendan, what do you know about sex?'

I nearly said: 'What do you want to know?' But I didn't think that he would see it as a joke.

'Oh, I know all about it, Daddy,' I said. 'It's in the science book I have for school. The reproductive system, they call it in biology.'

'Oh, right, son. But that's only the science of it, now. You know there's a holy side to it as well?'

There was a holy side to everything in our house. If prayers were pound notes, we would have been the richest family in Ireland. When we weren't going to Mass, it was Benediction. And all the other nights it was down on the knees in front of the sofa to say the Rosary. I should have had serious credit with God with all the praying I had done in my twelve years. But when I asked Him in that moment for a freak wave, like in *The Poseidon Adventure*, to come and carry me away, the Bank of God was shut.

'When a man lies on a woman and puts his thing into her, it's a sin unless they're married,' he went on. 'Do you know that son; a big, big sin?'

'Oh I do, Daddy. Father Seán taught us all that in religion class.'

'Fair play to Father Seán. I hope now you're behavin' yourself in his class. He's the best priest ever this parish had. He's the man'll get us a new chapel built.'

'Oh I am, Daddy,' I said. 'I'm no bother to Father Seán.'

'Good man yourself. But do you know what else is a big sin, son?'

I just wanted it to be over, like when you've got a toothache and you can't wait to get to the dentist, even though you know it's going to be horrible.

'Doin' it in the hand,' he said.

Doin' it in the hand? What was he on about? I was confused for a split second. Then two things dawned on me. She had told him, no question about that. And I realised that he was putting a name on the thing that I did not have a name for. And he was telling me that it wasn't just shameful: it was sinful.

There was a big dirty black cloud down over the chapel the following Saturday morning.

'You're in for it now, you thick lump,' said the Virgin Mary.

She had a cross look on her white alabaster face. I was on my knees underneath her, waiting for the confession queue to die down. Normally I looked forward to confession, especially the buzz I got coming out of the box with my soul wiped clean: the buzz of being back in God's good books. But I was anxious. My father said that what I was doing was a sin, so I would have to tell it. And if it was as big a sin as he said, I might be on my knees all day doing my penance.

'Does not compute! Does not compute!'

The damned robot was whirling around my head like a lunatic.

'How could it be a sin?' he asked. 'Who does it hurt?'

I dug my knuckles into my temples to shut him up. The idea that my father could lie to me was too scary to imagine.

'But what if...?' said the robot.

It was my turn next in the box. I worked out a compromise. I would chance not telling it. If I didn't get the buzz, then I would know that it was a sin and I could tell it next time. If I came out with the buzz...No! I just couldn't go there.

The shutter drew back. Father Seán nodded.

'Bless me Father for I have sinned. It's been two weeks since my last confession. I said some curses and I told a few small lies to my friends and I spoke back to my mother and ahmm...'

'Go on, Brendan,' he said.

He knows it's me, I thought. I panicked.

'Ahmm...ahmm....'

'Did you have impure thoughts since your last confession?'

Oh fuck, they must have told him, I thought. I felt the slimy claw crawling up my spine and popping my head wide open. Father Seán could see all my thoughts. I could feel him rooting around inside. There was no point in lying to him.

'Ahm...I found a magazine, father, with bare women in it and I've done it in the hand.'

'This is very serious, Brendan. Do you still have the magazine?'

'Yes father.'

'These magazines are not just against the laws of God. They are against the law of the land. You could be in serious trouble, Brendan. Have you told your parents?'

'No, Father.'

'But you brought this filthy and dangerous thing into their house?'

'Yes, Father, I didn't mean to father. I didn't know.'

'You don't want your parents in trouble with the guards do you, Brendan?'

'No, Father.'

'Bring the thing to my house. Four o'clock. Do not tell anyone. Do you understand?'

'Yes, Father.'

Father Seán answered the door. Far from being cross, he had a friendly smile on his face.

'Come in, Brendan,' he said and closed the door behind me. 'Hang up your coat on the rack. It's lovely and cosy in the sitting room.'

He put his hand gently on the small of my back and smiled at me again.

'Have yourself a bun,' he said. 'I'll just see if the kettle's boiled.

Do you have the thing with you?'

I took the magazine out from under my jumper. He took it from me without opening it. I felt a huge weight lifting off my shoulders.

I sat down on the sofa. There was a blazing turf fire in the grate and fairy cakes on the coffee table with icing on them. I started to pick at the hundreds and thousands on the icing. I took a bite out of a bun. This particular bad episode is coming to an end, I thought.

Father Seán came in with a teapot in one hand and the magazine in the other. He opened the magazine at the middle pages.

'Now, Brendan,' he said. 'Do you really like these pictures?'

His voice wasn't scolding. It was calm and controlled, not the least bit embarrassed like my father's had been. He was talking to me man to man. I felt ashamed and guilty. I decided to be honest.

'I kinda did, Father,' I said. 'Before Daddy said that doing it in the hand was a sin.'

'I see.'

He turned away from me, like he was thinking things over. He took a set of keys from his pocket and went to a writing desk, his head bowed, like he was praying for my lost soul. He chose a key and unlocked a drawer in the writing desk. He took something out of the drawer and turned back to me. The way he moved reminded me of Nero in *Quo Vadis*, when he ordered the Christians to be fed to the lions. He put a heavy brown cardboard envelope down on the table.

'Here are some other pictures, Brendan,' he said.

He slid a magazine out of the envelope and opened it up on the table in front of me.

'Let's see which you prefer, shall we?'

I couldn't speak. The slimy hand was squeezing the life out of my lungs. His pictures were making me more frightened than I had been when I saw *Dracula* and that's as scared as I had ever been in my life. Father Seán's pictures were of naked men. They had willies up their asses and in their mouths. He sat down beside me on the sofa.

'Well, Brendan?' he said. 'What do you make of those boys?'

And the fear I had known only seconds before was magnified a thousand times. Father Seán, the closest man to God in our town, the man who had the power to wipe my soul clean, put his hand on my willie.

'Does not compute!'

The robot tried his best to get me out of there. I jumped up off the sofa and bolted for the door. But he tripped me. He rolled me over on to my back and sat on my chest. I tried to fight him but my body had turned into cotton wool. He gripped my head between his knees.

'You're a disgusting little pervert,' he said. 'What are you?'

The smell of his aftershave was overpowering. It was Old Spice.

I didn't get home from my secret place down by the river until after dark. I still had the taste of him in my mouth. Daddy was fixing the motor on the washing machine.

'Where were you til this hour?' he said. 'I thought I was going to have to call the guards.'

I didn't need him to be angry with me. What I needed was for him to tuck me up in bed and go and give Father Seán a clip so he would never come near me again.

'Fa-Fa-Father Seán….'

'Father Seán what? What in God's name is wrong with you?'

I didn't have the words. The robot was gone.

'Father Seán did…he put my….Father Seán did it in the hand in my mouth.'

His face darkened. He slammed the scullery door shut as if he was afraid my words would have all the demons of hell coming through it at any minute.

'Don't let me ever hear you say anything like that about a priest.'

I didn't feel the slap. His words killed whatever feeling I had left in me.

Lunar Ladies

Phyl Herbert

Her tea trolley is set. The cups are placed upside down on saucers stacked on plates. Annie's Sunday soirées are an event written into the social calendar of the many women of her acquaintance. But this Sunday is different. It is the Sunday before the New Year and only her two best friends are invited.

The bottom shelf of the trolley hides the sweet delicacies that will follow the egg-sandwiches. She looks in the big gilt-framed mirror, pins back the grey curl on her forehead with a silver slide and then adjusts her dark glasses. She scans her figure from head to toe. Annie is wearing her favourite dress given to her by her best friend, Hilda. A knitted dress of deep royal blue fits snugly on her four foot ten inch frame. The pink pom-pom slippers complete the outfit. She smiles at her reflection. The doorbell rings.

'Coming,' she hums. She lifts the buzzer phone on the wall of her living room, opening the front door.

'Hope I'm not too early?' Hilda kisses Annie on the cheek.

'Delighted to see you, Hilda. I'm more than ready.' Hilda places her fur coat carefully behind the white settee and hands Annie a small box. 'A few éclairs for later.'

The low table in the centre of the room is covered with paper cuttings of theatre reviews and a green, leather-bound diary containing her meticulous daily entries. The afternoon light slants through the broad windows of Annie's living room. It is an old purpose-built apartment block, one of the first built in Dublin, not far from the sea in Dun Laoghaire.

The bell rings again and Annie lifts the buzzer phone.

'Come in if you're good-looking, entréz s'il vous plaît.'

Annie and Bonnie embrace each other.

'We're all here now,' Annie says. '*That time of year thou mayst in me behold!*'

Annie makes this pronouncement as if she is about to say Mass.

'You look terrific, Bonnie. Your hair is getting blonder and you're getting younger-looking. I swear to God, I don't know what you're doing to yourself,' Hilda says almost accusingly.

Bonnie looks in the mirror and chuckles. 'I have to say, folks, I'm sorry I didn't go blonde years ago. Whoever said youth is wasted on the young was right.' Bonnie speaks with the energy of a bossy P.E. teacher. She dresses much younger than her years. Today she is casual; her blue jeans and tennis shoes accentuate her athletic figure.

'You're dead right there, Bonnie. We were such innocents that we didn't even know we were either young or good-looking. What sort of eejits were we?' asks Hilda.

'You're still looking good, Hilda,' says Bonnie. Hilda is wearing a black trouser suit with a white crisp cotton blouse underneath. A string of pearls frames her neckline.

'Will you stop fooling yourself. When you get to my age the hairdressers have only one style for you and that's the Cauliflower Head of Curls.'

'Hilda, you have to demand more of them.'

'Are you playing any tennis these days, Bonnie?' Annie asks. Bonnie is looking into the mirror and reapplying her red lipstick.

'Yes, Annie, I had a game this morning. I play with three other women and they would beat any young player off the court. Hard to believe they're in their seventies. They still have power in their elbows and strength in their swing. Their joy in the game has rubbed off on me.'

'How often do you play?' Annie is curious.

'Twice a week. I'd play more often if I could. But tennis is like sex – you can't do it alone.'

She looks at Annie for a response. She is warming up, trying a few shots. Annie smiles, lifts her small shoulders and swings back to Bonnie. Annie may be small but she likes to project large. She engages in dialogue as though she were pronouncing from a stage.

'Age is all about confidence.' She mulls over her words. 'Look at that director fellow – I can't remember his name – he is all over the tabloids. He must be in his sixties, going out with that young one. His own daughters are older than she is.'

Hilda is on the edge of her seat.

'Go on,' she says, urging Annie to continue. Hilda loves the theatre gossip but Annie will say no more. She has made her point. Hilda has seen two husbands to the grave.

'Sure I didn't live at all, got no pleasure out of them, I never knew which end of me was up. Don't ask me why I bothered marrying either of them.'

Bonnie and Annie listen in sympathy and say nothing. When Hilda was a young girl, her dark looks were compared to those of Sophia Loren. She and her sister were the first to be invited up to dance in the Metropole Ballroom in O'Connell Street. Her dancing days were short-lived. Marriage took away her dancing feet and after she gave birth to four children in quick succession, her likeness to Sophia Loren faded. So did her marriage.

'It was the thing to do back then,' Bonnie sighs.

'What was?'

'Get married.'

'You never got caught, Bonnie.'

'No, and look where it got me. My head was always in the moon. I don't know where my forties and fifties went. What was I doing for those years?'

The three women sit in the centre of the living room. The apartment was left to Annie by her aunt and uncle over forty years earlier. They were both Abbey actors and the room is a shrine to their memory. Framed photographs line up a gallery of remembrances. The walls are green. Annie likes to call it her green room. The acting heroes look down from every side of the room. Three white sofas surround the low table.

'Well, Annie, what did you see at the theatre festival this year?'

Annie takes a breath and rises in the chair.

'*The Crucible*. It was bleak. I left at the interval.'

Bonnie is surprised. She too had seen it. 'My God, Annie! Not again! You didn't go back after the interval?'

'No. I couldn't hear that fellow who played the father. He couldn't project. Actors can't project any more!' She sticks out her chin and fiddles with her hearing aid.

'I don't know, Annie. I enjoyed it. I think Arthur Miller is the master. None of those young ones know how to write a play any more. They're all full of rambling monologues now.'

Bonnie knew the theatre scene in Dublin. She spent most of her youth directing other people's talents. It was now her time to live her own life. Annie rises gracefully from her seat and goes into the kitchen. She is about to perform the tea ritual.

Hilda looks at Bonnie and smiles. 'We have to let her; it *is* her party.'

'How did your Christmas go, Hilda?'

'Mother of God, I'm glad it's all over. I was stuck in a corner at my niece's table and I thought I'd never get home.' Hilda is breathless. 'Do you know what they gave me? A single cup and saucer wrapped up in fancy paper with a blooming big bow on it. Now if that's not a reminder that I live alone, I don't know what is. I can't wait for the New Year.'

Annie comes back pushing her trolley to the centre of the room. Hilda turns up the three cups on their saucers and Bonnie pours the tea. The egg-sandwiches are eaten, and as always, someone says, 'Annie, you make the best egg-sandwiches in the world.'

The china cake stand at the bottom of the trolley is bedecked with Hilda's chocolate éclairs and Bonnie's Swiss roll. Both have to be sampled. Hilda takes a bite of chocolate éclair and looks at Annie.

'It's only here that I allow myself the pleasure.'

The three women laugh.

'Did you see Nigella last night?' Annie looks at her two friends for a response.

'No, what was she cooking?' Bonnie asks.

'I don't give a fig for what she cooks,' Annie says forcefully. 'I just love looking at the sheer physicality of her performance. She makes me feel hungry.' Annie blushes and tries to change the conversation. Hilda and Bonnie look at each other. They are used to Annie's crushes on attractive young women. Last year it was a young actress who performed in a lunchtime play in Bewley's. Annie travelled into town every day to see the play. But since her stroke a few months ago, she has become housebound. This year the objects of her desires are television personalities.

'Can I read out my poem before we start?' Bonnie searches in her big red handbag. 'It is called "Archaeology of the Soul".'

'Archaeology, what has that got to do with the soul?' asks Hilda.

'The past,' says Annie authoritatively.

'Can I begin?' Bonnie sits up straight and takes a deep breath.

'At the funeral of my youth
Only one offered a cushioned
Grave for my remains.
"Will you marry me?" he asked.
"No," I replied and then I died.'

'I know who you are talking about, Bonnie – that homosexual fellow. You had a lucky escape, believe me.'

'Finish the poem, Bonnie.' Annie commands.

'Now I am the big Oh...
And have opened up myself on the shelf.
I want to dance to the tune of sex
Have babies and catch up on myself.'

'My God, Bonnie, are you mad? How on earth could you have babies? At your age!'

Bonnie is uneasy at her revelation. 'I know what age I am, Hilda. It's just a fantasy, I suppose.'

There is an awkward silence.

'Now to the business that we have all been waiting for.' Annie stands up. She takes down the portrait of her aunt and uncle and turns their faces to the wall. Behind the portrait are sellotaped three sheets of paper. She passes a sheet to each woman.

The women read in silence.

'We can write our wishes for next year later, but would anyone like to talk about their last year's wishes?'

'Jesus, Mary and Holy Saint Joseph,' Hilda exclaims, 'if any of my children knew I did this, they'd have me certified.'

'You're not dead yet! Who is going to read out their wishes of last year?'

Annie is taking control.

'I will,' says Hilda. 'My number one was to lose weight and get more exercise. Well I didn't do too well there: I'm still the same tuppence ha' penny. My number two, to learn how to please myself more. My number three, to get away more often while I still can.'

'You did very well, Hilda. Haven't you been away a lot this year?' Annie interjects.

'Yes, I suppose so, but not with people I like. It was like being back at school, being told where to go and at what time to go. I didn't enjoy a bit of it. I only went on those trips because the bridge club needed to make up the numbers.'

'There was no pleasure in it for you, Hilda,' Annie says.

'Pleasure,' repeats Bonnie. She plays around with the sound of the word on her red lips. 'That is what it is all about, pleasure.' She laughs, turning a little pink. She faces Annie. 'Read out your wishes.'

'I'm still hosting my Sunday afternoons and inviting people I knew over the years who touched my life. My second wish was travel but, unlike Hilda, I can't travel now. Thank God, though, I still have my imagination. I can travel in my head, can't I? A girl can dream, can't she?' She chuckles, suddenly embarrassed at the thought of revealing her third wish.

'That's two wishes. What about your third?' Hilda asks.

Annie rises in her seat. She drops her chin and takes a deep breath. 'I'm a little reluctant to verbalise my D-E-S-I-R-E, as Bonnie would say. I don't feel confident about saying what my third wish is, not just yet, anyway. I'll wait until you read out yours, Bonnie.'

'All right, Annie, but there is no need to hold back with us. The three of us have kept the wishes our secret since the beginning. I'll read mine out.' Bonnie looks at her page of wishes. 'I have progressed a little since last year. My number one last year was like Hilda's: health and fitness. Thanks to my tennis partners for that. My second one was joy in my life.'

'Mother of God,' says Hilda. 'How do you parse that one?

'SEX, Hilda. PLEASURE, DESIRE. Call it what you like, that act of… Oh, I don't know what I'm talking about.'

There is silence. The room is trapped in time. The women are winding back the years.

Bonnie looks at the two women. 'It goes on until the grave.'

'What does?' Hilda asks beseechingly. Her eyes light up. It is as if Bonnie is holding the secret to the meaning of life.

'Desire, Hilda,' Bonnie says. She again plays with the sound of the word. She opens her mouth as if she is about to taste the word for the first time.

'Let's face it, where are we going to meet men at this stage of our lives? I thought about this very seriously until I came up with the answer.'

'Mother of God, Bonnie. You're not serious! You have not!' says Hilda.

'Yes, I have. The Internet. I took ten years off my age and registered myself under the name of Babs, a fifty-two-year-old active woman seeking suitable company.'

The silence in the room is now taut with contained excitement.

'Good on you, Bonnie,' Annie says. 'Please take us out of our misery and tell us all.'

'I got four replies. One man was in his sixties, too old for me; another was in his late fifties, also too old. So I replied to the man in his late forties, forty-seven to be precise, and I met him. We went to a lunchtime concert at the National Concert Hall.'

'Are you meeting him again?' Hilda asks breathlessly.

'I don't know, to tell you the truth. I don't know what to do with him. He sort of left me a bit cold.'

'Mother of God, I have heard everything now,' Hilda says. 'If I took ten years off my age and said I was sixty-four, would I have a chance?'

'Try it, Hilda,' says Annie. 'But I can tell you one thing: if I took ten years off my age and said I was seventy-four, I know I'd disappear and be vapourised in cyberspace – so I won't bother, thank you. Men are messy, anyway,' she says distastefully.

'Annie, we have yet to hear of your third wish. Come on, out with it,' says Bonnie.

'Promise not to laugh,' Annie pleads. 'I suppose since we are all being honest about our desires, I will put mine on the record. I would love Nigella Lawson to bring me breakfast in bed, then to join me under the duvet for a cup of tea. Just for once in my life. Now it's out – I've said it.'

Hilda puts her hand on Annie's shoulder and says, 'We can arrange that, love.'

Bonnie smiles at Annie. 'My third wish last year will be the same for next year and that is that we meet again with joy in our hearts.'

The wishes are made now and sellotaped on the back of Annie's aunt and uncle and the portrait is reinstated for another year. The business is completed and Bonnie and Hilda say their goodbyes. They leave the apartment facing the dark of the night, like two bookends with the coming year's wishes between them.

Annie pulls over a kitchen chair to the window to see her friends' departure. She waves regally to them as their car drifts away out of sight. *What a lovely night it is out there and what a lovely evening we had in here.* She looks up at the full moon through her dark glasses. *How could anyone believe that there was a man in the moon?* She smiles. *The moon is much more a feminine force.* She searches the sky for stars, but the moon is the centre of the constellation, the leading light. *Hello my beautiful moon. Make our wishes come true.* Giddiness takes hold of her and she now sings out again. Clapping her hands together, she applauds the moon. Forgetting that she is standing on a chair, she returns to her room to walk to the kitchen. Her little body crumples to the floor.

Annie wakes up in hospital. Both her wrists are broken. She cannot believe her eyes. Looking down on her is Nigella. Her gentle brown eyes soft and her heaving breasts covered in white satin.

'I'll have to feed you breakfast, Annie,' the young nurses' assistant says.

Annie smiles at her.

'Thank you, Nigella, you are so good.' She inhales deeply and closes her eyes.

A week after Annie's funeral, Bonnie and Hilda are taking the air on Dun Laoghaire pier. The pale blue of the sky merges with the sea, casting a gentle light on the harbour.

'She went so fast, poor Annie.' Hilda says, near tears.

'God love her.'

'You know, I swear to God she believed that Nigella was catering to her every need up until the end.'

'Her every need.' Bonnie ponders over these little words. 'None of us know what our every need is. Certainly I don't think Annie did.'

'I wouldn't be too sure about that now, Bonnie. She was never interested in men.' The two women walk to the end of the pier and look out to sea.

'Does this mean there will be no more wishes next year, Hilda?'

'We can't make them without Annie.'

'Well, the tide is hardly going to stop coming in and out because Annie is dead.'

'What is your every need, Hilda?'

'Will you stop going on about that, Bonnie, and grow up.' Hilda is becoming annoyed. She looks around making sure nobody is listening.

'Just as well Annie is not here.'

The tide of hope is fast running out in Bonnie's heart, but then

Hilda thinks of Annie's words: 'You're not dead yet Bonnie.' She smiles. And the tide rises.

Smugglers' Cave

Andrew Fox

I watched Aodh coming over from the direction of town. The fire stood between us, and my face burned looking at him. I had to squint to make him out, but that lolloping walk – even across the loose shingle beach and its bockedy piles of stones in the dark – was distinctive. I hadn't forgotten it. And I don't think I ever will. He swung a bag of cans by his side, and with every few steps his hand went up to his face, where a little red pinprick glowed: he had taken up smoking some time in the past five years.

This was something we tried to do every year on New Year's Eve: we would all meet up at The Smugglers' Cave, our old drinking place, to be together for the countdown. That year was meant to be a big one – five years since we had all finished school – so Louie had brought up a generator and his decks. We knew there would be no problem from the Gardaí: Chris was a year out of Templemore. One of the girls had brought up these big torches – reservoirs of gasoline encased in ornamental wicker – and we buried their bases in sand around the cave walls. There was a wick at the top of each, and we lit them and we could see.

When I arrived, it was just getting dark. Ross and Ger were already there, piling all the crap for the fire – which Ross had gathered from the builder's yard and Ger had gathered from the street – into a big heap a safe distance from the mouth of the cave. A few of the girls sat apart, holding themselves and rocking against the cold. The gennie was humming in the background and Louie was already at the decks, planning out his set; he always took that sort of thing very seriously. When the boys saw me coming, they shouted jeers at me – 'Missus let ye out, did she?' – because I had told them (unwisely) that I was to have an early dinner with Gwen at her parents' house before I could make it up.

'But I'll get there,' I had said. 'I wouldn't miss it. And she knows who's boss.'

'Yeah: her,' Ger had said.

Ross threw a paintbrush at me – 'Here' – and pointed at three tins of paint he had stolen from work. 'Make yourself useful – artist,' he said, but then they both came over and gave me a hug. The girls waved and went back to divvying up their vodka.

I had a bottle of wine with me – 'Fancy,' Ger said – but I had cans too. We finished the wine as we caught up, and I directed them in painting the cave: these big, animal and hunter paintings – caveman paintings like Ross wanted. I don't know if real smugglers had ever even used the place, but that was the name everyone knew it by. And the first night we had gone there, back in second year with Aodh's and Ger's older brothers, they had told us all these swashbuckling stories, and ghost stories to try and scare us, and the magic and mystery of them had made me so much want to believe the myths that I had never asked any real questions. Ross drew a big, angry-looking face and gave it a pirate hat. 'Smuggler,' he said.

I took a handful of water from the stream which trickled from the back wall of the cave, and slurped – I knew it to be fresh from the night I had spent yipped out of my mind and had to drink gallons of the stuff – then I washed my brush and pretended not to hear the other three sniggering. When we were finished, Louie rewarded us with a fat cone and we smoked it and drank a can each while admiring our handiwork. We sat beside the girls on the cold rocks, with a bitter smell rising from the piles of wrack heaped up and abandoned by the tide, with the sun turning the low parts of the sky pink, and the new fire crackling and streaming smoke in thick white ribbons. The wind whistled across the cave-mouth.

'Always said the place could use a lick of paint,' said Ross, his eyes running across the scenes we had picked out in red and green and blue.

'Looks gift in anyway,' Ger nodded.

'Yeah: deadly,' said Louie, with great effort, his voice weakened by trying to keep his chest full of smoke.

'Thanks,' I said.

'Here, Hungry-lungs,' said Ross, smacking Louie on the back, making him cough and splutter and the girls dissolve into nervous giggles. 'Give us that.'

Aodh and me look quite alike. I should probably say this now. That's where the confusion and the trouble started. And our names are similar: Aidan and Aodh. When Gwen moved to our school from Bruges, she had told her cousin, who was in Ger's woodwork class, that she liked Ger's tall friend with the long hair. Most of us had long hair back then, but only Aodh and me were tall.

'Aidan?' the cousin had asked. He could just as easily have said Aodh.

'I think so,' she had said.

And then Ger told me. And when he asked me would I be with her I said 'fuckin sure'. And then I had said it to Aodh as well. But of course by this time Aodh and her had met each other – they were in the same English class – and the mistaken identity had been sorted. They were already going out.

'Shit, Aidan. This is awkward,' he had said, rubbing his chin like he does, and then he explained it to me.

'Oh Jesus,' I had said; 'sorry,' embarrassed, as you can imagine. But he was very understanding about the whole thing, and we even got to the stage where we could laugh about it – a joke at my expense, but I preferred quiet derision to open hostility.

And me and Gwen got to be friends. We were partners for an art class project, where the six best students were split into three teams of two, and asked to design murals for the new wing of the school. It was awkward at the start, but I got over my mortification and we managed to get on. We found that we worked really well together too, and our mural – mine and Gwen's – won in the end. We did this big, blue, moody scene from *The Children of Lir*, since it was her favourite myth – her mother used to read it to her when she was younger. Both Gwen's parents are Irish. Her Da was in the diplomatic corps. She was born in Belgium and has a thick French accent.

Later on she'd say that she had liked both of us at the start, and that in fact both me and Aodh were… 'in the running' – I think was how she put it – from the beginning, and he had just happened to get there first. I'm not sure if I believe that, but it was during the time we worked together that things started to happen.

Louie was excited that Aodh would make it back. They were still in touch. Aodh had gone to England after school to study music… something, in a tech in Reading.

'Funny you live in the same country and you never see each other,' Chris had said to me once, because he didn't understand.

After college, Louie told me, Aodh had been playing in a band, touring the country and trying to get a label. They had a manager, who Louie said he'd heard of, and Louie had been over to meet with them a couple of times. They played a few gigs together: colleges, that sort of thing. One time he brought back a CD of Aodh's band's music, and it wasn't bad at all. They were all obviously very decent musicians, and Aodh wasn't a bad singer either. They just lacked originality. They sounded like everyone else to me.

We piled the last of the stuff on the fire – an old headboard, pallets, an office chair – and waited for Chris to get back from a beer run, holding out our hands to warm them and dancing a little to keep the blood flowing. Ross had his arm around a girl's waist. I'd never seen her before but she reminded me of Aíne Ní gCarroll –maybe she was her little sister. Louie couldn't stop talking about how excited he was that Aodh was coming but Ross and Ger stayed silent, out of loyalty to me, I suppose. Maybe just out of awkwardness.

I got a text from Gwen at about half ten, when most of the people had arrived already, when Louie was pumping hard techno out into the night and people were already hammered and dancing around the fire or running naked into the sea. It said:

Hope u hav fun 2nite. Dnt drnk 2 much. Tell a I say hi. Love g. X

Ger saw me reading. 'Who's that?' he asked.

'Gwen,' I said.

'Oh,' he said. 'Message from the war office? And how're things on that front?'

'Fine,' I said. 'We've got a gallery interested. We've been trying to collaborate more often recently. Kind of audio-visual installation…' But he broke me off with a wave.

'Right, right,' he said. 'Sorry skip, but you lost me there. I'm happy for you though.' He was still wearing a suit, and expensive-looking wood-soled shoes, even on the sand and rocks. He tucked his feet under him as he smoked, then he passed the joint to me.

'How about you?' I said. 'Any scéal?'

'Ah, working away.'

'Any – '

'No, no. Nothing like you. Not while I'm still young.' He took out his cigarettes and called for Louie, who threw over the dope. The action made him lose track of the mix, and for a moment the two records ran uncomfortably together. Louie grabbed at his earphones and gave us the finger.

'I'm a free agent at the mo,' Ger said, taking no notice of Louie, or his finger, or the car-crash sounds of the decks. I made a face. Ger formed the papers into a curve, split the cigarette, flicked his lighter and held the flame to the little brown chunk. 'Never mind that fucking perfectionist,' he said.

I watched his fingers. 'And work?' I said. 'How's work?'

'Grand. I'm getting rich.'

'That's good to hear,' I said. 'Good someone is.'

When Aodh arrived over, I looked away and pretended I hadn't been watching. He put his cans down beside me without even noticing.

'Hi,' I said.

'Oh. Hi.'

'How's –' I started, but Ross was calling Aodh's name from the back of the cave and Aodh was only too glad to turn and go to him. It was eleven-oh-six by the clock on my phone.

'You made it just in time,' I heard Ross say as he hugged Aodh, put his arm around his shoulders and led him over to a group of people.

'The drawings are great,' Aodh said. 'Who did them?'

'Aidan,' Ross said, leaning his head over Aodh's shoulder to look at me. It was a strange, emotionless look, as if all he wanted was to see me.

'I'm going over to say hi,' Ger said, and he got up, and left me on my own with his joint. 'Howiya, rock star?' he said.

I got another message from Gwen:

Hope u havin a gud nite. Mom and da fitin. Wish I cud b der wit u. Happy new year. G.

Aodh and Gwen broke up before the Debs but he still took her. We all went in a limo from his house and the two sets of parents – Aodh's and Gwen's – were very matey with each other. Aodh's Ma had put on a big spread: cocktail sausages and pizza and burgers, and salads for anyone who might be interested. He had told her not to, because there was a meal at the thing, but she had said it was for the family, and that he didn't have to eat if he didn't want to. I don't think either set of parents expected them to stay broken up. They got on well with each other and I'd bet you they were already thinking about what it would be like to be in-laws.

At the Debs though, Aodh and Gwen had a huge fight, another one, one of their biggest. And they had become famous around school, over the year and a half they were with each other, for big ones. Aodh was blind, mummified drunk, and he had tried to kiss her and she shrugged him off. I was standing at the bar drinking tequila with Ross when I saw her get up to leave, and I heard – the whole place heard – her shouting at him: 'No. I told you. I told you.

We're done.' It seemed like a pretty cold-hearted thing to tell a guy, so final, especially after his parents had welcomed yours like royalty and he'd shelled out eighty-five quid for a tux, and God knows how much more for a limo, so when he came over to us I tried to talk to him.

'Jesus,' I said. 'That looked pretty rough. Are you all right?'

But he just pushed past me to the bar and said 'Not now. I don't want to get into this now. Not with you.' Then Ross looked nervous and bought another round of tequilas and we drank them together quickly in silence.

I ended up getting sick right on the bar, and then nearly having full-blown sex on the sink in the gents with Áine Ní gCarroll, who had been my date, and who had made it very clear to me, in no uncertain terms, that she was a nymphomaniac. But I got brewer's droop and had to make my excuses.

I went out for some air and to smoke and to clear my head after that, and to wonder what the hell Aodh had been talking about. I found Gwen crying, sitting on a step at the hotel's goods entrance. I sat down beside her and gave her my hankie for her face. She was shivering and I gave her my jacket. She thanked me. I ended up hugging her. And she told me that she had always liked me and all.

Things seemed to me to be getting out of hand. A few lads from The Close had come over and were taking it in turns to jump over the low part of the fire – 'Run amok!' One of them slipped and landed in a heap, and his head missed the fire by inches. His friends laughed, spilled beer, shouted 'Steo, your head's gone!'

I got pretty drunk. I smoked three cigarettes end-to-end and watched the party go on around me. Some of the guys and some of the girls were skinny-dipping together. Ross had lost his shirt, was dripping wet but didn't seem to notice the cold. Ger was smoking a joint with a few girls. Louie had taken a break from the decks and he was sitting, like all the rest of my friends, in a loose circle around Aodh. Someone had brought a guitar along and Aodh was playing it – I recognised it as the song he had sung at our graduation, and I felt like puking from the sentimentality, but all the others were singing along – Ross especially, in that screeching atonal voice he gets when he's properly hammered.

'Are you listening to this?' I said to the girl standing nearest me. She had only just shown up. She had long, pink dreadlocks, and I had overheard her telling someone that she was a circus acrobat. Chris was telling her about the history of the cave: all this romantic shit about men living outside the law hundreds of years ago, battling the English on their own terms and what have you, giving himself the horn and hoping, I'm sure, to get into her kacks. I spat on the ground as I spoke. And she wheeled around, shouting in a thick English accent.

'Did you spit at me? Did you just fucking spit at me?'

I flushed, alarmed by the drunken craziness that was so clear in her eyes. 'No I…' I stuttered.

'Aodh!' she shouted.

Aodh stopped playing. The singing went on without him for a moment but then that stopped too. Aodh stood up, holding the guitar by the neck.

'Frankie, hi!' he shouted, smiling big and waving.

'Aodh! This guy' – she pointed at me – 'This guy just fucking spit at me!'

Ross and Ger and Louie stood up. The rest of the circle turned around. Hard faces. I looked at her, at Aodh, at all of them, and behind them at the cave walls flickering in the torch – and fire-light – the stick figures with their stick spears hunting stick animals – the long, jumpy shadows on the walls.

'Wigs on the green!' one of The Closers shouted.

Aodh took a step forward, still strangling that guitar. Its heel battered a rock, and sounded a note, and the echo told me how quiet it had gotten. Aodh was about twenty feet away, and we looked at each other for a long minute with her screaming her head off now, and someone somewhere laughing like a lunatic, and the sea rolling, and little bits of ash, and little sparks come crackling up in the fire and carrying on the breeze in the air between us. We watched each other like that – Aodh and me. Then I held up my hands, and turned, and left.

Halfway to the road I realised I was still carrying a can. I hurled it out over the sea and listened for the splash. But I couldn't hear it. I stumbled and turned my ankle on the big loose stones, swore sorely through gritted teeth. The night was cold away from the fire. I folded my arms around my body, unfolded them to blow on my hands. I couldn't hear my friends anymore, just the steady tumbling of the sea and the odd shout from I couldn't tell where. I limped to the foot of the steps, climbed up onto the road, holding a cold, metal handrail whose surface the sea air had eaten into rough carbuncles. A family across the way were having a party. I could see them through the window, standing all in an arm-linked circle, all wearing bright paper party hats.

Ten, nine, eight, seven...

I shivered, took out my phone and dialled Gwen's number, but it was no good: everyone in the country was trying to ring their loved ones, and the network was down.

The Authors

Carmen Cullen, former Head of English in Coláiste Dhúlaigh, Coolock and Director of the Oscar Wilde Autumn School in Bray, is now concentrating on her writing. She has published *Class Acts: Original Plays and Workshop Themes for Secondary Schools*, Folens Educational, 1994; *Sky of Kites: Children's Poetry*, Kestrel Books, 1998; and *Under the Eye of the Moon: Children's Poetry*, Mercier Press, 2001. Other publications include many collections of children's writing. She is a children's storyteller and a writer in prisons. She has had writing residencies for children with Wicklow and Dun Laoghaire Arts Offices and Poetry Ireland Educational. A novel for adults is underway.

Rachelle Dolan was born in Seattle, Washington. She received a degree in History with honors from the University of Washington in 2007. She is currently working on a novel and a series of short stories.

Niall Duff is from Clonsilla in west Dublin. After graduating from NUI Maynooth in 2003 with a B.A., he did postgraduate research in Anthropology. He works as a Philosophy tutor and an English teacher. He is currently studying for a Philosophy PhD in the area of emotion. He lives in Dublin and is working on his first novel.

Emily Firetog was born in Brooklyn, New York twenty-three years ago. She graduated from Swarthmore College in 2007 with High Honors and now works for the Dublin literary magazine *The Stinging Fly*. She is currently working on a collection of short stories.

Andrew Fox is from north County Dublin. He received his undergraduate degree from UCD, and plans to return there to begin graduate research. He is currently at work on a series of short stories. He lives in Dublin.

Phyl Herbert was born and lives in Dublin. She worked as both a teacher and theatre director. Her published work includes plays and textbooks for the teaching of drama.

John Holten has lived and worked in Paris, Berlin, Dublin and Oslo. His fiction and writing on art have appeared in various publications and websites, most recently in *Circa* and the *Cúirt Annual*, 2007. He is currently writing a novel.

Viv McDade was born in Northern Ireland, grew up in Zimbabwe and lived in Cape Town and Amsterdam before moving to Dublin. She has a teaching diploma from the University of London, a degree in English and an honours degree in Psychology, both from the University of South Africa. Prior to her fictional life, she lectured at a teacher training college, made pots and worked as a business consultant.

Naoimh O'Connor writes short fiction. She was part of the first Irish writers' group to produce an author-driven theatre production (The Ten Commandments Reloaded, in SS St John's Blackbox Theatre, Temple Bar, 2006). She was born in Laois, lives with one foot in southern Italy and the greater part of her mind in a white house by the ocean.

Maria Pace grew up on a farm in Virginia, USA. Among other things she has worked as a newspaper reporter, an English teacher, a painting instructor and an illustrator. The only thing she knows about her future is that she would like to keep on writing until she is an old, old lady.

Ruth Patten was born in Dublin in 1983. She graduated from Trinity College with a degree in Classical Civilization and Italian in 2006. She has worked as a receptionist, a journalist and selling sweets and newspapers. She also worked as a tour guide in Rome at the Vatican museums and is of the opinion that you can never see the Sistine Chapel too many times. She is currently working on her first novel.

Philip St John was born in Dublin. His stories have been published in New Irish Writing and broadcast on RTÉ. His play *The King of Beverly Hills* was short-listed for a Bewley's Short Drama Award. He is currently finishing *Crazy Baldheads*, a novel set in Jamaica in the 1980s.

Charlie Stadtlander hails from both coasts of the United States. He was brought up in New Jersey and lived most of his adult life in Seattle, where he studied writing at the University of Washington. He once rode a bicycle across Europe and refuses to let anybody in this country know that he is half-Irish, because he says it doesn't really seem to matter.

Mark Stewart has worked at many jobs, including barman, census enumerator, dishwasher, DJ, film-maker, gardener, labourer, lecturer, lifeguard, salesman, screenwriter, script reader, tour guide, TV director and waiter. His most significant writing success to date was the screenplay for the cult Irish film *Accelerator*. He lives in west Cork where he is an art event organiser. He enjoys cooking and parties.

Monica Strina is the spoiled fourth child of a great family. She grew up under the Sardinian sun and graduated with high honours in Foreign Languages and Literature in 2002. A year spent in Dublin as an Erasmus student convinced her that she must go back to Ireland and to one of its inhabitants in particular. Her first novel, *Quattro Volte Sette Lune*, was published in Italy in 2004. She is currently working on a novel in English and learning to play the violin in between hikes. Her gang of crazy friends is one of her many blessings. She is an incurable chocoholic.

Mary Turley-McGrath grew up on the Galway/Roscommon border. After graduating from UCD, she moved to Letterkenny, Co. Donegal, where she worked as a teacher of English and Communications. Her first poetry collection, *New Grass Under Snow*, was published by Summer Palace Press in 2003. Her poems have been successful in national competitions and she has been short-listed twice in the Scottish International Poetry Competition. In autumn 2004 she won the Annie Deeny Award. Her work has appeared in magazines and anthologies, and has been broadcast on RTÉ. She is currently working on a second collection.